Serving Up Hex

CRESCENT MOON MYSTERY #5

TARA LUSH

COVER DESIGN BY LOU HARPER/ COVER AFFAIRS

EDITED BY THE AUTHOR BUDDY

MAP ILLUSTRATION BY SARAH WAITES

For Lou

CYPRESS GROVE
FLORIDA
Coven House
Oliver's House
Bicentennial Park
Marigold Wentworth Boardwalk Park
Police Station
Ice Ice Baby
Haunted Hearth
Astral Attic
Library
PUBLIC LIBRARY
POLICE
Crescent Moon Inn
Enchanted Eternity Park

One

On hundreds of websites, perimenopause is described as the "change of life," and is usually accompanied by a photo of a group of women clad in earth-toned, natural fabric clothing. They're strolling on a beach and smiling beatifically, as if the hassles of middle-age can be solved with a good, hearty walk in salt air.

In reality, here is what midlife looked like: my friend Renee Zinn and I slouched in a booth at Ice Ice Baby, our preferred local coffee shop in our town of Cypress Grove. We were sweating, pink-faced, and droopy. I was in khaki shorts, a pink T-shirt sporting the words THE MOON MADE ME DO IT, and hopelessly unhip Teva sandals. Renee was in a long, sleeveless, green tie-dye dress and dung-colored Birkenstocks.

"Is it hot in here?" she asked, fanning her face with a menu.

"It is to me, but no one else here looks moist, so I dunno." I glanced around. Two elderly women at a nearby table were staring intently at a tarot card spread. Most everyone else looked younger than us, and their skin was both tight and dry. Ugh. I felt like a sweaty troll.

"Please, no. Not the M word." Renee smiled and pressed her plastic cup of iced coffee to her forehead. "I suppose I should tell you why I asked you to meet me here."

"Is this about the festival?" I immediately went over my mental to-do ticker. This week, I had a full house at The Crescent Moon Inn, the bed and breakfast I'd inherited last year from my Aunt Shirley. I'd also promised to make several dozen cookies for our coven's pre-Solstice tailgate party. That was a couple of weeks away, though.

The entire town was abuzz about the Summer Solstice Festival. The town was not only putting on its usual big event, but would also formally commemorate the pardoning of Constance Winters, a local witch wrongly imprisoned for murder in the 1960s who died behind bars before her name could be cleared.

The case had gained renewed attention when a determined group of high school newspaper students investigated the decades-old evidence and finally proved her innocence. While the Crescent Moon Inn buzzed with summer visitors and local business owners like me scrambled to prepare the usual festival treats, there was a more somber undercurrent to this year's celebration — a sense of long-delayed justice finally being served, unfortunately too late for Constance herself.

"Well, no. It's a little complicated." With a napkin, Renee wiped her forehead from the moisture left behind from her cup.

It was always a bit complicated with Renee, who I adored. She was the co-leader of the Sisters of Hecate, a coven for Generation X-aged witches here in town. Since I was a relatively new member and eager to participate, I'd spent quite a bit of time with Renee on various projects. Well, that and the fact that we'd recently banded together to defeat a rogue witch here in town.

Like I said, the coven offered many choices and opportunities. Beyond the obvious spell work, I'd also signed up for bake sales, how-to seminars, and a summer floral arrangement class.

"Wait. Is it about the pop-up dining thing?" I'd agreed to host some VIP foodies at the inn shortly after the solstice festival. Renee, ever the connection-maker, had introduced me to the organizer.

She shook her head and cleared her throat. "Okay, here goes. Will you join the coven's pickleball team?"

Well, that wasn't expected. I knew this was one of the many activities offered by my witchy group. Just one that I wasn't particularly keen on.

"Um."

So far, I'd loved the sessions I'd taken part in, especially the "Intro to Tarot" class and "Familiar Care 101: From Litter Boxes to Loyalty Bonds." But everything I'd done had been indoors. Activities that involved sitting in air conditioning. Things out of reach from the punishing heat and humidity. It was summer, after all. My first here in Florida. And it was kicking my butt. I loved living here, but my word.

I pressed my hand to my clammy chest. "Me? What? You're joking, right?"

Although I'd become more active since moving to Cypress Grove last year, I wasn't what anyone would consider athletic. That was the benefit of owning a historic inn near downtown — almost everything was within walking distance. I was killing the step counts on my smart watch.

"You lived in California," Renee said easily, making me think that she'd anticipated my question and also my resistance to her idea. "You'd be a great addition to the team. Oh, and it's an indoor court. I forgot that important detail. It's not like we're going to play outside in Florida in June."

"So, you're *not* joking about pickleball. Hmm. What does California have to do with anything?"

"You mentioned playing tennis once." She tapped her temple. "Like a steel trap. I don't forget things."

I laughed. "I played tennis in high school, and sporadically over the years with my ex-husband. But never pickleball."

Renee clapped, her evil eye bangle bracelets jangling. "You're perfect! See? I'll send you some YouTube videos about the rules. You'll pick it up in no time."

"I think our definitions of perfection in ball sports are vastly different. Why do you need someone so badly? I thought the pickleball team was full. Didn't I read that in the coven newsletter a couple of months ago?"

"You did. But one member had knee surgery, another is out of town for the summer, and..." She sighed. "Liz."

I reached for my iced coffee cup, which was perspiring. The air in here had to be on the fritz. "Oh, right! She's on the team."

"She's my partner. Or was."

"It's been, what, six weeks since her operation? Hasn't she recovered? It seems like she has. She's back to work at the store."

Liz had undergone emergency gallbladder surgery recently. Everyone in the coven had been taking turns bringing her casseroles, healing spells, and reading material. She owned the Astral Attic, a metaphysical shop in town, and a few coven members had even stepped in as salesclerks. I'd kept Liz well stocked in kombucha and homemade Snickerdoodle cookies.

Renee shook her head as a blast of air from an overhead vent hit us. "Her doctor wants her to not do any strenuous exercise for another month or so. But don't worry. It's not *that* strenuous. Well, it would be for Liz in her current state. But not for you. Anyway, please? It's only a few games and I promise it's so fun. Low-key, as the kids say. We'd be partners. I know we'll have a blast."

"I don't know." I took a sip and swallowed, finally feeling a little cooler. "Pickleball seems like a lot to learn. I don't know if my brain can handle much more, since I'm spending a lot of my free time studying my new psychic powers. And you know I'm not exactly the sporty type."

Renee leaned forward, her big green eyes fixed on me. She pressed her palms together in a pleading gesture. "Amelia, pickleball is amazing! Everyone gets addicted to it. And I'll sweeten the deal and give you a private astral projection lesson!"

I felt a familiar warmth of wanting to support my friend, but also a twinge of guilt. At my core, I was a people pleaser. I was trying to get better about saying no, but when Renee looked at me like that, I found it hard to reject her plea for help.

Plus, the astral projection class would be kinda cool.

I reminded myself that it was okay to help friends while still maintaining healthy boundaries. It was all about finding balance, something I sure as heck hadn't mastered in my twenties, thirties, or most of my forties, come to think of it. Since I'd recently celebrated my forty-eighth birthday, my goal was to head into my fifties with some kind of sanity and equilibrium.

"Well..." I started, still uncertain.

"Come on, Amelia. It'll be awesome! And you'd be doing me a huge favor. Please? We'd be playing doubles against another team. A couple of local guys." Renee's tone, slightly higher pitched, told me something else might driving her to ask for this favor.

I sighed, torn between not wanting another thing on my to-do list and the desire to help. Renee had been through a lot in recent years, even more than I had: the death of her husband and a layoff from a career she'd loved. On top of that, she worked three part-time gig jobs to make ends meet, and handled the coven responsibilities with humor, grace, and efficiency. She barely had time for her main passion, taking aura photos with a vintage polaroid camera.

This month, she was leading the coven, since the other co-leader was in Sweden at a wicca retreat. Why Renee wanted to fool around with pickleball and add another thing to her plate was beyond me.

Being her partner would probably make her life easier, though. One less thing to worry about.

"Okay, tell me more," I said, softening. "But this isn't some kind of double date setup, is it? Because you know I'm with Oliver."

Saying that aloud shocked me. I was forty-eight and had a *boyfriend*.

Renee's eyes widened. "Oh, no! Nothing like that. It's only a game, I promise. Maybe two. But it's not a date or anything. For you."

"Then why do you need a partner? Can't it wait until Liz is better?"

Renee's cheeks took on a pink tinge. "I met someone at the new racquet club. His name is Jack, and he asked if I'd like to play a doubles match."

"Ah, so that's it." The pieces were falling into place. A grin spread on my face. "Why not have dinner with him? Or coffee?"

"I did have coffee with him, the day after we met at the club. We went to Bella Brava."

That was the upscale, fancy coffee shop in town with the eight-dollar lattes. "Oooh, swanky. And? How was it?"

She inhaled, and a hopeful smile spread on her face. "Actually, it was pretty nice. He chews with his mouth closed, he asked questions about me, he didn't check out the hot barista, and he has a dog. We talked for two hours and would have stayed longer, but I had a piano lesson."

"I have to admit, that sounds promising. But the pickleball match? Why are you so insistent about playing against him? That's a weird date."

Renee smirked. "Because, my friend, I want to see how he does when he competes against women. It'll tell me a lot about his character and whether I want to share a meal with him."

I couldn't help but snort. "That's actually pretty smart."

"I know, right?" Renee beamed. "If he's a sore loser or gets all macho about beating 'the ladies,' then I'll know he's not worth my time."

I took another sip of my coffee as I pondered. "Tell me about this guy."

"I don't know too much. He looks age appropriate. Maybe a little older than us? Late fifties, early sixties. I didn't ask his age. Handsome, silver hair, really fit. Impressively fit. Relatively new to town, from what I gather. He really loves pickleball, so we have that in common."

"Job?"

She tugged at her ear. "Not sure. But I did see that he drives a new car. An electric one."

"Hmm. Might be promising." Both of us knew it was difficult finding men our age who were single, employed, and interested in women older than twenty-five.

She sighed and looked down at the table. "I know this seems a little desperate, begging you to be my pickleball partner. I'm sorry. I've been lonely lately. I hate even admitting that."

"No, I get it. When you meet someone who's interesting and possibly sane, you want to give it a chance."

"Augustus told me to give it a chance."

My eyebrows shot up. "Come again?" I wasn't sure what her late husband had to do with any of this.

"He came to me in a dream recently."

From what I'd heard, Augustus had not only been much older than her, but he was a renowned wizard. I hadn't wanted to pry for more details, but secretly, I was fascinated by the entire thing. Renee rarely spoke of him. "Really?"

She nodded and lowered her voice. "He told me that this was a year of transformation for me. He said I should embrace all of the change."

"I see."

"Here's how I interpreted the dream." Renee pushed her curly hair out of her face. "I took that to mean I should say yes to more things. That's what I've been trying to do. It's why I've been throwing myself into whatever the coven asks. And whenever someone invites me to do something, I do it."

Part of me wanted to give Renee a pep talk on balance, the one I repeated to myself every few days. It seemed like she was doing quite a bit already. But she was a far more accomplished witch than me, and it wasn't my business to interfere with her dream realm conversation with her dead husband.

"So, saying yes to Mr. Silver Pickleball Fox is another way to say yes to new things?"

She nodded, her expression sober. "It sounds silly for a fifty-five-year-old woman. I know that. But the day I met Jack? Augustus came to me in a dream that very night and told me I was on the right path."

Well, that sure sounded like kismet to me. Or serendipity. Or fate. I still wasn't entirely clear of the distinction of the three. Maybe this pickleball dude was her destiny. Who was I to stand in the way of all that?

"Okay," I said finally. "I'll do it. But only once, okay? I can't commit to a whole pickleball season or whatever. I don't want to get caught up in travel tournaments. I remember my daughter's soccer team."

I shuddered at the memory of spending every weekend driving to high school games.

Renee squealed. "Thank you, thank you, thank you! You won't regret it, I promise. It's going to be awesome! And Liz said she'd be there with us to act as our coach, er cheering squad."

"Yeah, yeah," I grumbled, but I couldn't help smiling at her excitement. "So, when is this game supposed to happen?"

"Day after tomorrow." Renee winced. "Is that okay?"

I groaned. "This Saturday? I don't even know if I have proper shoes. Do I even need special shoes? And I know nothing about pickleball."

"Don't worry! Just wear sneakers. I'll send you some YouTube videos, and we can practice a bit before the match. Or, wait, no." She reached for her phone on the table and scrolled with her thumb. "I've got lessons, and I'm supposed to do a big transport for the blood bank. But you'll be totally fine. I promise. And we'll get you an outfit. I'll drop one off or have someone swing by the inn."

I shrugged and grinned. "It's all good, I guess. I'll muddle through, as I always do."

"Thanks. I appreciate you."

I smiled, already wondering what I'd gotten myself into. But as I looked at Renee's pleased expression, I knew I'd made the right decision. Sometimes, being there for a friend was worth stepping out of my comfort zone. And who knew? Maybe I'd even enjoy pickleball.

Stranger things had happened in Cypress Grove, Florida.

Two days later, I was standing in the hallway of Pickled, waiting to play my first game. When I'd read about this place a couple of months ago in the local newspaper, I assumed it was a new bar, and was eager to check it out.

But no, it was an upscale, private, pickleball-themed racquet club, not an artisan cocktail joint. I guess I had to count my blessings, though. It was blissfully air conditioned, and we *could* be playing outside in the Florida inferno.

Renee was here, and Liz was too, as our cheering-squad-slash-coach. She'd given me a quick rundown of the game's history on our drive over. I hadn't realized that the two of them were so wild about the sport — they used all sorts of pickleball jargon and inside jokes.

"Seeing you in your outfits, I'm so bummed I can't play." Liz winced as she sat on a bench. She was clearly still sore from her surgery, but looked adorable in her lime green velour tracksuit.

"You feeling okay?" Renee asked her.

"You sure you shouldn't be home, resting?" I added.

Liz shook her head. "It takes me a little while to get going in the morning. But that's middle age, you know? You both look so cute. Let me see the back."

Renee spun around so the hem of her skirt twirled. On the back of her stretchy, bright yellow dress was a black silhouette of a bee. Our team's name was the HoneyBees, probably because a handful members of the coven owned beehives, and the group used a cute, cartoon version of the insect as our mascot.

"Looks perfect," I said.

"Yours fits great," Liz said, appraising me. School bus yellow wasn't normally my color, since I had strawberry blonde-ish hair, but I wasn't going to argue. Somewhere between starting perimenopause, a brutal divorce, and moving across the country, I'd stopped caring as much about what I looked like.

I scratched my side, near my armpit. Like a monkey.

Something felt off with the built-in sports bra in this dress. "It's a little itchy in one place. In fact, I'm going to use the ladies' room before the game. I want to investigate what's causing this."

"We have plenty of time," Renee said. "Make sure to top off your water bottle."

"Definitely. You're going to sweat," Liz warned.

"Good idea. I'll be right back."

I hustled toward the bathroom, grateful for a moment alone to compose myself before my first official match. Of course, I got lost because Pickled was so enormous. In fact, I couldn't believe a swanky athletic franchise like this had chosen small town Cypress Grove for their new location.

The spacious lobby gleamed with polished marble floors. I passed sleek, modern furniture in muted tones of grey and blue, a juice bar serving fifteen-dollar organic smoothies, and a pro shop that looked more like a boutique in Miami.

I paused for a second and darted into the shop, making a beeline for the sale rack. There was some cute stuff here. In the background, soft techno music played.

"That rack is what's left of last season," a clerk called out.

"Thanks." I inspected a cute black getup. If I had more time, I'd try it on. The tag said fifty percent off, but the original price wasn't immediately clear. I quickly moved to the regularly priced merchandise and reared back when I saw the price tag.

Two hundred fifty bucks for a pickleball dress?

I slunk out of the shop.

This whole place baffled me. While charming and quaint, Cypress Grove was far from the sophistication of South Beach. It was known as the Psychic Capital of the World and was packed full of witches, mediums, reiki masters, astral projectionists, aura experts, warlocks, and possibly even werewolves (I believed this was a rumor, since I hadn't seen evidence of them).

But someone, somewhere, was apparently trying to turn our eccentric town into the regional mecca of pickleball, since this was Pickled's first central Florida outpost.

I wasn't sure how that would work out, but I was relieved to finally locate the spacious, clean, bathroom. It was more like a lounge, with fluffy towels, hand lotions, and mouthwash. I could only imagine what membership in this place cost; I was here on a day pass.

There was no one else inside, and I exhaled when I stopped in front of a full-length mirror. Something was very off about this outfit. It bunched in a weird way right where I was itchy.

As I twisted and turned, trying to get a good look at that spot, I noticed what was bothering me. The built-in bra elastic of the coven-assigned pickleball uniform was drooping like week-old lettuce, folding and digging into my skin.

"Great timing," I muttered, tugging at the elastic. It had completely lost its stretch, probably during the voyage through my washing machine. So much for reading the care label. Liz had assured me this was a new uniform, but I was having my doubts.

I rummaged through my purse, praying to the fashion gods for a miracle. Lip balm, mints, old receipts, a baggie of palo santo sticks in case I needed to purify a space on the fly. Why did I have so much junk in here? Finally, my fingers closed around something small and metallic, along with some loose stones. A-ha! A safety pin, probably left over from an abandoned craft project.

"The MVP of my pickleball game," I whispered, holding the pin up like a trophy. I flipped up the dress so I could get access to the bra part. For a few seconds, I fought with the Lycra material.

Contorting myself into a position that would make a yoga instructor proud, I managed to get the elastic somewhat aligned. I finally maneuvered the safety pin into place, and didn't stab myself in the process.

Once it was secure, I gave my reflection a onceover. The fix wasn't pretty. The outline of the safety pin was evident and lumpy, but it would hold. At least, I hoped it would. The last thing I needed was for the girls to flop around as I was lobbing a serve.

Did players in pickleball lob? I wasn't certain. My entire knowledge of the sport came from one YouTube video and a wordy, confusing email from Renee — and Liz's history lesson in the car. Both women had assured me that we were going to play a team that was at a beginner level, like us.

I wondered about the guy who invited Renee. Would he look like one of those fit older folks I'd seen wandering the halls of Pickled in their expensive designer outfits?

Since no one was in the bathroom, I lifted my arm. On Liz's recommendation, I'd started wearing natural deodorant. First, she had suggested a crystal, which was sloppy when wet, had a weird, rough texture, and had failed miserably in the odor-fighting department.

This new stuff looked like traditional deodorant but smelled like I'd rubbed a crayon on my skin. It was an improvement on body odor, I supposed. It wasn't perfect, but it was a small step in being more mindful about what I put on my body. These days, I found myself questioning many things I'd accepted without thought before, always with an eye on how my choices affected both myself and the world around me.

I took a quick whiff. Crayon. Oh well. Could be worse.

I went to the eco-friendly water dispenser and filled my bottle. This place sure was nice. Maybe I'd love pickleball and this would be *my* new hobby. I imagined myself in the cute outfits in the boutique, my hair longer and in a jaunty ponytail that swayed as I thwacked the ball. I hadn't been a bad tennis player in high school.

As I headed for the door, feeling confident in my MacGyvered outfit, something caught my eye. Tucked in the dirt of a potted fern in the corner of the stylish bathroom lounge was a pickleball paddle.

"Well, that's an odd place for that," I muttered, reaching for it. The paddle was sleek and new, its rubber grip still pristine. It looked expensive, certainly nicer than the borrowed one Renee had lent me. Honestly, it looked like Renee's paddle, with a purple whoosh on the flat part. Maybe she'd left it in here, since she'd used the bathroom not long before me.

The moment my fingers closed around the handle, the world tilted. A familiar dizziness washed over me, and I braced myself against the marble countertop. It was a psychometric vision, an ability I'd gained since moving to Florida.

The bathroom faded away, replaced by a hazy vision. I couldn't quite place where I was — perhaps Pickled, maybe somewhere else. Two men were arguing, their voices muffled as if underwater. Through the haze, I caught a flash of perfectly manicured fingers gripping the paddle tightly, long nails painted a deep wine red. Someone was eavesdropping on this conversation. Or maybe was part of the conversation? It was difficult to tell.

"You keep bringing in these cheap knock-offs," the man snarled. "This isn't what we agreed to."

"Keep your voice down," the other man hissed. "I know what I'm doing. Just stick to the plan."

I gasped, snapping back to reality. The vision dissipated like smoke, leaving me clutching the sink with one hand. I dropped the aluminum paddle as if it was made of molten-hot iron, and it clattered to the tile floor.

"Oh yikes," I whispered, my heart racing. "That's not good at all."

My psychometry had never steered me wrong before, but I desperately hoped it had this time. Whatever I'd just witnessed felt ominous, to say the least. I stared at the paddle.

As I was debating, I heard the door to the bathroom swing open. I held my breath.

Three

"Amelia? Hey, the guys are here and we're about to start." It was Renee's voice.

"Okay, be right there."

The sound of the door closing and the long hiss of my exhale echoed through the empty bathroom.

I reached for a navy-blue washcloth — the club used those instead of paper towels — and picked up the paddle, making sure my skin didn't come into contact with the cursed thing. Since moving to Cypress Grove and discovering I possessed this power, I'd come to understand a few of its quirks.

Namely, I could stop the visions if I had a barrier between my fingers and an object. This is why I sometimes used cleaning gloves around the inn, which was once owned by my aunt. There wasn't enough time in the day to have multiple visions of Aunt Shirley's past and get everything done.

Usually, I could go to stores and tune out the background noise of the visions as I connected with items. Things that I had come to think of as "high touch objects" — like doorknobs, menus, chairs in public places — had so many sensory details that they often blended together in a faint tingle on my fingertips. But if the object had strong enough energy from one person, I was going to feel, smell, see, taste, and experience everything in a vision.

I deposited the paddle on the bathroom counter, next to the mouthwash and lotion station. Then I scurried out, hoping that I didn't look pale, sweaty, or freaked out. When I returned to the hallway, I noticed that Liz and Renee were talking to two guys.

As I got closer, I recognized one of them: Dominic Harper, a local art gallery owner I'd met a few months back. The other guy was tall, muscular and had gunmetal gray hair. He was handsome in a generic kind of way. I assumed he was Renee's new friend Jack. I pasted on a smile, trying to shove the vision into a far corner of my mind.

"Ah, there you are!" Renee called out, waving me over. "We were about to send a search party."

I walked up to the group. Dominic was talking. "...and so then I was about ready to begin the Ironman triathlon..."

Dominic's eyes swept over me without a flicker of recognition, clearly annoyed that my presence had interrupted his story. I recalled our first and only encounter at his art gallery opening a few months ago, orchestrated by my well-meaning but meddlesome mother. Clearly, the memory hadn't stuck with him as it had with me.

He did that thing where he quickly looked me up and down, determined that I was too old, fat, or useless, and glanced over my head, searching for someone who he deemed more interesting.

"Dominic, Jack, this is our friend Amelia," Renee introduced. "She's filling in for Liz today."

Dominic nodded politely, but I could tell he was already losing interest, if he ever had any. "Nice to meet you, Anna."

"Amelia," I said, suppressing a sigh. He was one of those men who treated middle-aged women as though they were invisible. When I last saw Dominic, he couldn't get away from my mother and I fast enough because a beautiful young thing had caught his eye.

The man standing next to Dominic stepped forward. "Nice to

meet you. I'm Jack Reeves," he said, offering his hand, his light brown eyes crinkling at the corners. "Dominic's friend. You're the inn owner?"

I shook his hand, appreciating his firm grip and direct gaze. At least someone acknowledged my existence, but I still was skeptical of his character since he was buddies with Dominic.

"Nice to meet you. Yes, I run the Crescent Moon Inn."

"Oh, I've heard good things about that place," Jack replied, seeming genuinely interested. "I actually suggested it to some friends who are coming to town later this year."

"Thanks, I appreciate that."

"Have to look out for our business owners in town. I'm trying to get to know more people."

Jack and I chatted for a bit about being new to the area, and both agreed Cypress Grove was a great small town with lots to offer.

Renee, ever the enthusiast, clapped her hands together. "Well, now that we're all acquainted, shall we head to the court? Amelia and I are about to make our debut as the newest pair representing the HoneyBees."

She whirled around to show them the bee on the back of her uniform.

"Love it," Jack said, grinning.

Dominic sniffed. "We're ranked at a four. How about you two?"

I felt my stomach drop. So much for playing against beginners or retirees. Dominic and Jack both looked fit and eager for a serious game. Dominic especially had a predatory grin that told me he was not here for a friendly match.

"Oh," I managed, trying to keep the dismay out of my voice. "Well, we're... uh..."

Renee jumped in. "We're still working on our rankings. Amelia here is a tennis convert, so she's got a mean topspin, but we're still getting used to the kitchen line and dinking."

I nodded enthusiastically, grateful for Renee's quick thinking.

"Right, exactly. I'm adjusting to the smaller court and the no-volley zone. It's quite different from tennis."

Dominic looked skeptical. "I see. Well, perhaps we should start with a practice game to warm up. We wouldn't want to overwhelm you with our power serves right off the bat."

"That sounds perfect," Renee chirped. "We're always eager to learn from more experienced players. Right, Amelia?"

"Absolutely," I agreed, silently marveling at how diplomatically Renee handled the situation. As we made our way to the court, I leaned in close to her. "Thanks for the save. I owe you one."

Renee brushed my shoulder with hers. "Don't worry about it. Remember, if all else fails, aim for the kitchen. They can't volley there."

I mentally scanned back to the videos I watched. What the heck was the kitchen again? And as far as I was concerned, the only dink was Dominic.

We followed the men down the hall and through a door to our reserved court. The indoor pickleball spaces were impressive —pristine and well-lit, with high ceilings and state-of-the-art flooring.

The blue playing court was marked with crisp white lines. Retractable nets divided the space into two regulation-sized pickleball courts, though only one was set up for our game. Everything smelled new, like paint and plastic.

While Renee and Dominic talked about who would serve first, I pretended to inspect my paddle while thinking of the vision I'd had earlier.

Liz sidled up to me. "Are you OK?"

"Yeah, I'm fine. Why do you ask?"

"I don't know. You seem a little off."

I stifled a sigh. Liz was unusually perceptive these days, and I wondered if she was coming into her powers — I'd overheard someone at the coven say that especially after anesthesia, middle-aged women often had a surge of psychic energy. It was why so many women in our coven discovered their powers after hysterectomies or knee replacement surgery.

"No, I'm fine. I'm a little nervous about this game since I've never played before. That's all." I shot her a manic smile.

She nodded, but I could tell she didn't quite believe me. "You're going to need to stay on guard with those two," she said, eyeing Jack and Dominic.

"Will do," I said. "I thought this was supposed to be a friendly, fun game, not something competitive."

Liz stepped a little closer and motioned for me to do the same. I did, and she grabbed my paddle, holding the flat part between two hands like it was a sandwich. I could have sworn she was infusing it with some sort of magic. I was about to ask when she piped up.

"That guy? Jack?"

"Yeah?"

"Renee's interested in him. They had coffee. And I think the feeling is mutual."

"Yeah, she told me about their date. He seems okay."

"They met here when we were playing together. It was during a happy hour at the rooftop bar. What do you think of him?"

My eyes grew wide. "They have a rooftop bar?"

"Don't get your hopes up. It opens at four and it's only nine-thirty in the morning."

"Crap. Well, Jack seems okay. I guess Renee wants to wow him with her pickleball prowess."

"Something like that. I'm not sure he's the right one for her. I get weird vibes. Stay alert."

I nodded, unsure of what to make of her observation. Liz was into community theater and tended to be dramatic at times.

"Okay everybody, let's play! Get in position." That was Jack, his voice friendly yet commanding. At first glance, he seemed to be a good match for Renee — he was age appropriate, his clothes were clean, and he had a nice smile.

Whether he was truly single, employed, and emotionally available remained to be seen. Liz's hesitation about him made me a little skeptical, but so far, he seemed fine.

I had to admire Renee's plan, though. Playing against him *would* tell us a lot about how he handled himself around women. If he lost, would he be gracious? If he won, would he gloat?

We would soon find out.

I thanked my lucky stars that I didn't have to deal with any of that stuff. I'd been dating a local professor, Oliver Everhart. It was more than just "hanging out," as my college-age daughter would say. Still, I hadn't pressed him on taking our relationship to the next level, and neither did he. We'd had a conversation about being exclusive one night, and since then, hadn't mentioned anything about the future. Which was fine with me.

Probably because both of us knew that the next level for folks our age was marriage, and I wasn't in any way, shape, or form ready for that.

Oliver was as kind as a summer day was long, and, unlike some men who were dating or even married to witches in town, encouraged my metaphysical journeys despite not having any abilities of his own. He also had a job, his own house, and a beautiful singing voice, especially when he played Cure songs on his guitar.

I took my place on the court as Renee had instructed. It was on the left side, behind the non-volley zone, which I now remembered was the "kitchen." Being an innkeeper and the former owner of a cookie company, you'd think I'd have committed that to memory.

"We're serving first," Renee said, smiling at me, then sneaking a glance at Jack, who winked at her.

I noticed she looked a little flushed, her cheeks rosy, her eyes a little wild. Goodness, this was a lot to take in in one day. A new sport. A wardrobe malfunction. My friend having a crush on a man who looked like he stepped out of a Viagra commercial. Plus a psychic vision to top it all off.

This was fun, though. These were my people. This was my new life.

I needed to get my head in the game and do my coven proud. Then I caught myself. While I cared about Liz and wanted to play well for the coven's team, I knew it was okay to also play for myself, to enjoy the game in the moment. It wasn't selfish to find joy in my own experiences. No need to get competitive.

"Come on, come on, come on," Liz shouted from the sideline. She clapped her hands a few times. "Let's start building some hurt bombs, ladies."

Yikes. Okay. Liz was serious about this. So much for rejecting competition.

I grasped my paddle, feeling the grippy texture of the handle as I stood in position. To my surprise, it felt good, natural. Getting back into racquet sports was a positive thing. I'd buy a cute pickleball dress, but maybe not in that expensive boutique. Target probably had some.

When I looked up, I saw Renee and Jack on either side of the net, grinning and shaking hands.

"If we win, you pay for dinner," she said.

"And if we win?" Jack asked.

Renee raised one eyebrow saucily. I'd never seen her flirt with anyone, and I had to admit it was pretty cute.

Across the net, Dominic smirked, his black paddle gleaming in the overhead light. Note to self: if I did get into playing, I'd steer clear of men like him. Or, no, I'd kick his butt on the court. That would be satisfying.

"Ready, Amelia?" Renee moved to me and whispered.

I nodded, while Renee served underhand, as required in pickleball. She sent the neon yellow plastic ball arching over the net. Jack returned it with a soft thwack that barely cleared the kitchen line.

I rushed forward, my old sneakers squeaking against the court as I lunged for the ball. My paddle connected with a satisfying pop, and I angled it to send the ball cross-court.

Dominic surged forward but stopped short of the kitchen. The ball whizzed past him, landing just inside the sideline.

"Well played," Dominic said, a hint of surprise in his voice.

"Nice one!" Liz cheered as we reset for the next serve. "Hit into the strike zone, witches!"

The rally continued. It was surprising how much had come back to me from my tennis days, though pickleball required quicker reflexes and a softer touch. The hollow pop of ball against paddle was an oddly satisfying sound, and we slipped into a rhythm that almost made me forget the earlier, disturbing vision. Almost.

Dominic and Jack were good players, I had to admit. But in my totally amateur estimation, Renee and I were holding our own. We made an excellent team, in fact.

As Dominic wound up for a powerful drive, he sent the ball whizzing to my side of the court. As I smacked the ball with the paddle, I felt a familiar tingle in my fingertips. Oh dear. What was going on? It almost felt as though I was about to have a psychometric vision.

The sensation vanished in the blink of an eye. Odd.

The four of us continued to volley, the ball flying back and forth across the net. The men grunted as they hit the ball. That was the only indication the two men were exerting themselves. Meanwhile, Renee and I were starting to sweat. Stupid menopause.

Again, Dominic lobbed the ball high, aiming for my backhand. When I struck it, once again I had a split-second flash of a vision. It was of a pickleball paddle whizzing through the air, but it inspired the same feeling I'd had in the bathroom — fear.

$$\mathcal{F}our$$

I fumbled and missed the ball, sending it right into the net.

"No worries, Emmy. It happens to the best of us," Dominic said, his tone somewhere between reassurance and superiority. Why couldn't he get my name right?

Liz let out a loud strangled groan. "It's okay, *Amelia*." I noticed she put particular emphasis on my name and said it a little louder. "It's okay. Stay focused."

Dominic flashed a smile, looking like a big, arrogant jerk.

Jack served, starting another rally. When he struck the ball toward Renee with a powerful drive, I saw the ball almost glow faintly purple. Whoa. What was going on here? The ball appeared to hang in the air for a fraction of a second longer than it should have, and it was all the advantage Renee needed.

Renee stepped into position, her paddle a blur as she countered Jack's drive with a precise dink. The ball barely cleared the net, dropping softly into their kitchen before either man could react.

"Impressive," Jack said, his eyebrows raised. "You ladies are full of surprises."

Renee and I high fived, and I felt a little spark from the palm of her hand transferring onto mine. I suspected Renee was using some kind of magic. She was a powerful witch who knew how to conjure spells that were beyond my comprehension.

I wasn't sure this was entirely legal in the world of pickleball, but I figured all was fair in love and in Cypress Grove. Renee and I shared little smiles.

We worked up to a good rhythm. Jack smashed the ball and it whizzed past Renee, landing near the sideline with a soft thud.

"Out!" Dominic called immediately, his voice sharp and certain.

I froze, certain that I'd seen the ball clip the line. "I don't think so," I protested, "that was definitely in."

Renee backed me up. "I saw it hit the line. That's our point."

Dominic shook his head, his nostrils flaring. "It was clearly out. I had the best view."

The four of us converged at the spot, tension crackling in the air like static electricity kissing a dryer sheet. I could feel a buzz beneath my skin as annoyance bubbled inside me.

"Look," Renee said, pointing to a faint mark on the court, "you can see where the ball landed. It's touching the line."

Dominic snorted. "That mark could be from any ball. It was out, end of story. I have an eye for detail, you know. Comes with the gallery business."

He and Renee locked eyes, neither willing to back down. Jack laughed nervously. I did as well, though mine sounded more like a strangled cat. The friendly atmosphere of the game was quickly evaporating.

Liz joined us from the sideline. "I also think it's Renee and Amelia's point. And I've been playing pickleball longer than any of you. But in the spirit of good sportsmanship, why don't you all replay the point? That's the fairest solution if we can't agree."

"I've been playing for years. Even took lessons from Joel Pritchard himself. I know what's what, and I don't think that's necessary," Dominic said, his tone firm. "We called it out. You need to respect the call."

"Come on, man." Jack seemed almost embarrassed by his

friend's stubbornness. He clapped Dominic on the shoulder. "Let's let them have it."

Dominic looked at Renee, then me, his gaze lingering a moment too long. "You witches think you can get away with anything, don't you? But not this time. The ball was out, and that's final."

I bristled at his tone, feeling my own temper threaten to boil over. If there was one thing that made me come unhinged, it was entitled, arrogant men. Probably a byproduct of living with my ex for decades.

Still, I didn't want to ruin the day or the game, even if the idea of showing up Dominic was becoming increasingly tempting. He reminded me a little too much of my ex-husband, in fact. The only way to deal with a man like that was to ignore him.

"Why don't we take five and grab some water to cool down," I said, trying to diffuse the tension.

Dominic harrumphed and stalked off while still holding his paddle. Renee, Jack, and I all looked at one another.

"He's been a little stressed lately," Jack said. "Business stuff."

Renee and I nodded. Jack mumbled something about needing to use the facilities and slouched out, obviously embarrassed by his teammate's behavior. Who could blame him? Still, I was disappointed that he didn't acknowledge Dominic's arrogant behavior. A strike against Jack.

I turned to Renee. "What was that all about?" I hissed.

She shook her head. "I've heard some not so pleasant things about Dominic around town. I had no idea he'd be here today. I feel bad, because I thought Jack played with someone else here at the club, a nice older man who sells insurance. If I had known he was teaming up with a guy like that, I would have said no, and I definitely wouldn't have invited you. I'm sorry this is your first pickleball experience."

I waved her off. "It's fine, I'm kind of used to dealing with men like him. Plus, it's been a fun game. I do like it, actually. A lot."

"I'm so glad. Hey, I'm going to get more water and use the ladies' room," Renee said. She smiled at me and Liz and walked out, leaving the two of us in the now empty, cavernous court.

"Geez Louise, I didn't like the way Dominic spoke to us," Liz said, her fingers wrapping around the top of the net. "Guys like him…"

"Seem to think they're entitled to get what they want, when they want it? And if a woman says no to them, they act like a toddler?"

"Yeah. That."

I moved closer to Liz and lowered my voice. "Something weird happened in the bathroom, before we started playing. And the same thing happened while we were playing, too. Well, sort of."

"I knew it! You had that strange look on your face when you came out. Like you're fighting some fierce gas."

"Is that what I look like after I have a vision?"

"Sometimes. But don't worry about it."

"It was so odd." I gave her a quick recap of my psychometric vision, my stomach churning all the while.

"Do you think you saw Dominic hit someone with a pickle-ball paddle?"

I lifted my shoulders. "I don't know who I saw, or what I saw. But it seems awfully strange that I felt a similar sensation every time I hit one of Dominic's balls. Ugh, that sounds bad."

We both cackled, and then I continued. "I didn't notice it happening when Jack hit the ball. But I can't be sure, because everything happened so fast."

Liz pondered this for a moment. "The four of you had a really good volley going. I think it would be difficult to discern the vibes from a ball, don't you?"

"I would think so. But I'm still pretty new at all of this. I'm still surprised that I can have visions of things that happened decades ago. The other day, I picked up one of my aunt's old books and saw her drinking iced tea on the porch of the inn on the same day Elvis died. I wish there was a way to control my power, or at least use it in a productive way."

When I first came to town, I might have kept these thoughts to myself. Now, I was learning to embrace this newly awakened part of me, while still considering how I could use it to help others.

The corner of Liz's mouth quirked up. "That will come. But let's try to get through this game without any more fights."

"Good plan," I said, though I couldn't shake the feeling that something was off.

I decided to change the subject, mostly because I didn't want to overload my brain with thoughts of my psychic powers and what I might — or might not — have seen earlier.

"I'm excited about tonight's street festival. It sounds super fun. Are you sure you're feeling well enough to run the booth with me? How are you really doing? I'm sure we can get someone else from the coven to help if you're not up to it."

"No, I'm okay. It's only when I move a lot in certain ways that my surgery incision hurts or itches. I've also been using a special tea that Marisol made for me, and that seems to be helping with the pain. I'll make sure to get a nap later today. I actually am happy to get out this morning, and tonight. I've been bored out of my mind at home."

"I'll bet. You usually never stop moving."

Marisol was another friend of ours in town. Although she was a witch — a tea witch to be specific — she was not a member of our coven. She had her own membership in a couple of different clubs, one for Boomers and one for women of the Caribbean diaspora since her roots were in the Dominican Republic.

Liz and I chatted about Marisol's magical tea ingredients for a while, until Jack returned. He joined our conversation.

"What kind of business are you in?" I asked, figuring it would be a good idea to know more about the guy if Renee was so interested in dating him. I liked to look out for my friends. Most of us had been on several, if not dozens, of terrible dates, and we all had an unspoken rule in the coven to back each other up if needed. That included doing due diligence on unknown men.

"I'm an investment banker," he said. "I feel a little out of place with all of you here in Cypress Grove. You all do such interesting, exciting things."

By now Renee had joined us. "What's exciting?" she piped up.

Jack beamed at her, and I had to admit, his eyes lit up while he stared at her. "I was just saying how all of you do such cool things and I'm in a boring profession. An investment banker doesn't have the cachet that running an inn or a new age shop or an online metaphysical healer does." He pointed at each of the three of us as he listed our professions.

"You might not have the cache, but I'm guessing you pay your mortgage on time," Renee said laughing.

"Yeah, being a witch doesn't always provide a steady paycheck," Liz said.

The door from the hallway opened and Dominic burst in. "I'm ready to kick ass," he said. "Let's get this game started."

I noticed Jack and Renee exchanging coy smiles while Dominic took a long guzzle from his water bottle. Some of the liquid ran down his face and onto his T-shirt.

We all assumed our positions again, and I thought it was especially gracious of Renee to allow Dominic to serve the first ball. As we took our places, I felt a chill go through me. The paddle in my hand suddenly felt heavy, and I couldn't shake the memory of my earlier visions.

The game resumed and quickly ramped up in intensity. Dominic's serve whistled past me, barely giving me time to react. I managed to return it, sending the ball arcing high over the net. Jack lunged, his paddle connecting with a resounding thwack. The ball ricocheted between us, a blur of neon green against the court's blue surface.

Grunts and squeaks of shoes on the court filled the air as we darted back and forth. Sweat began to bead on my forehead, and I could feel my shirt sticking to my back. Despite the physical exertion, I found myself hyper-aware of every move Dominic made. His aggressive style of play seemed to mirror his personality.

Renee and I fell into sync, anticipating each other's moves as we volleyed against Jack and Dominic. The ball pinged back and forth, neither side willing to concede a point. With each hit, I braced myself for another vision, another glimpse into something sinister. But nothing came.

As the intense rally continued, I realized I wasn't experiencing more visions. The ball felt ordinary each time it connected with my paddle, devoid of the eerie sensations I'd felt earlier. Had I imagined the whole thing?

Dominic executed a particularly aggressive shot, sending the ball rocketing towards me. I managed to return it to Dominic's side of the court, barely. But he missed it. Then I heard a sharp intake of breath.

Looking across the net, I saw Dominic's face contort in shock. His paddle clattered to the ground, followed by his body. As if in slow motion, he crumpled to the floor with a sickening thud, his eyes wide and unfocused. He let out a long, guttural exhale. It sounded like air coming out of a balloon.

"Oh my word," I gasped.

For a moment, we all stood frozen in disbelief. Then reality crashed in.

"Dominic!" Jack shouted, rushing to his partner's side.

Renee and I exchanged horrified glances. Dominic lay motionless on the court, his chest eerily still. Jack peered into Dom's face, checking for a pulse. Renee joined him. I stood rooted to my spot out of absolute shock.

"This is bad." Jack swore aloud. "Can someone call 911?"

Liz dashed over to her purse, which was sitting atop a small table in the corner of the room.

"How can I help?" I said, my feet suddenly in motion, racing toward Jack and the fallen Dominic.

Somehow, in my frenzy, my body seemed to move faster than my brain could process. As I sprinted across the court, my foot caught on the metal post at the end of the retractable net as I was trying to squeeze between it and the wall.

I felt myself losing balance, my arms flailing in a futile attempt to stay upright.

The world tilted sideways as I ricocheted off the post and fell, the blue court rushing up to meet me. The paddle flew out of my hand. I hit the ground hard, the impact knocking the wind out of me. But that wasn't the worst of it. As I landed on the floor, I felt a sharp, stabbing pain in my left side.

For a moment, I lay there, dazed and struggling to catch my breath. Then the pain in my side intensified, and I rolled onto my back with a groan. I looked down and saw a small spot of red blooming on my yellow uniform, right where the stabbing sensation was coming from.

With shaky fingers, I felt around. To my horror, the safety pin holding my built-in sports bra had come undone in the fall. The sharp point had pierced my skin, leaving a small but painful puncture in the side of my torso. I reached down the front of my dress and fished out the pin.

"Amelia!" Liz cried, rushing over. "Are you okay?"

I winced as I tried to sit up. "I'll be fine. Don't worry about me, worry about him."

I gestured toward Dominic, who hadn't moved. His eyes were peeled open and looked weirdly glassy. I'd seen that look before, and it always meant one thing.

Death.

Five

Dominic's chest wasn't rising and falling like a normal, living person. It struck me that this was one of those crisis moments that we all really needed an adult in the room, and yet, we were the actual adults, and we needed to do something fast.

Jack was still beside him, trying to find a pulse. He pressed his index and middle fingers to Dominic's wrist, then his neck.

"No, no, no," Jack muttered, his voice barely above a whisper. "This can't be happening. Okay, buddy, here goes. Come on. *Come on.*"

We all watched as Jack tried to do mouth-to-mouth. It looked nothing like what I'd seen on TV. Then again, what did?

Renee paced back and forth, her cell phone clutched tightly in her hand. "There's no signal in here," she said, her voice cracking. "Why can't I get a signal? It's probably because I have that cheap phone carrier. Ugh."

I pushed myself up to a sitting position, wincing at the sensation of the pinprick. The bleeding from the pin had thankfully stopped, leaving only a small red stain on my yellow uniform. It seemed trivial, considering the situation unfolding before me. Quickly I fastened the pin to my skirt.

"Liz," I called out, my voice sounding strangely calm despite the panic welling in my chest. "Can you try calling 911 or go find someone from the club? Maybe you have cell service?"

Liz nodded, her face pale as she fumbled with her phone. "I'm on it," she said, her fingers flying over the keypad. After a moment, she spoke, her voice steadier than mine would've been. "Yes, we need an ambulance at Pickled, the new racquet club on Highway 98. There's been... there's been an accident. A man's collapsed."

She paused and held the phone away from her ear. "Is he breathing?"

Jack, who was now attempting chest compressions, yelled no.

As Liz relayed the details to the dispatcher, I watched Renee sink to her knees beside Jack. Her eyes were wide with disbelief, her hand hovering uncertainly over Dominic's eerily still body. Was she trying to do Reiki? It seemed that much more jarring because only seconds ago, he was in motion.

He'd been *alive.*

"I don't understand," she whispered. "He was fine. How could this happen?"

Jack stopped the CPR, his gaze fixed on Dominic's face. The shock seemed to have robbed him of speech, leaving him looking lost and vulnerable.

"Keep trying," Renee urged, and he nodded and started the compressions again.

"They're on their way," Liz shouted, breaking the silence and startling Jack. "I'm going to find someone who works here. Maybe they have a defibrillator or a doctor or something."

Before I could respond, she was gone.

I pushed myself to my feet, ignoring the twinge in my side. As I approached Dominic's body, the hair on my arms stood up. The memory of my earlier visions flashed through my mind.

The argument, the paddle swinging through the air, the bad vibes. Now someone was dead. Was any of it connected?

My gaze fell on Dominic's discarded paddle, lying just beyond his outstretched hand. Something tugged at the edges of my consciousness, urging me to pick it up. I hesitated, glancing at Jack and Renee, but they were too focused on Dominic to pay attention to me.

I reached for the paddle. My fingers closed around the handle, and immediately, I felt that tingling sensation creeping from my fingers up my arm. The world around me began to blur.

As the present fell away, I braced myself.

The vision that engulfed me was hazy, like looking through a fogged-up car windshield. I was in a locker room, eerily similar to the one I'd been in earlier. The air felt thick with tension, and I could make out Dominic's figure, his face contorted with anger.

"You think you can walk away?" His voice dripped with venom. "After everything I've done for you?"

He gripped the paddle, and I could feel the rage coming off him. Never had I felt this kind of rage myself, nor in a vision. It was disturbing.

I strained to see who he was talking to, but the other person remained frustratingly out of focus — and silent. As I was about to catch a glimpse of Dominic's target, the vision shattered.

"Ma'am! Are you alright? You're bleeding."

I blinked, disoriented, as reality crashed back around me. For the third time today, I dropped a paddle and it clattered to the floor.

Two employees in black Pickled uniforms had burst into the room, one carrying a first aid kit, the other a portable defibrillator. The taller one with the kit was staring at me, his eyes fixed on the small bloodstain on my stretchy yellow sports dress.

"I'm fine." I wasn't though, since I was still reeling from the abrupt end to my vision. "It's a pinprick. Please, help him." I gestured toward Dominic's motionless form.

"You don't look too good, ma'am," the tall guy said. "You're pale."

"That's my face." I shook my head and waved him off.

As the guy moved to Dominic's side, I glanced down at the paddle on the floor. Its surface was worn, the grip slightly frayed at the edges. How old was this paddle? The vision I'd seen could have happened days ago, or even weeks. Pickled had been open for a couple of months now.

Or my vision could've been from something more recent. Like a half hour ago.

The uncertainty made my stomach spin, and the coffee I'd guzzled before I came here threatened to creep up into my esophagus.

More employees poured in and clustered around Dominic. Someone cut open his T-shirt, while the other checked for a pulse.

"No pulse," the tall employee announced, his voice tight. "Starting CPR."

As he began chest compressions, his colleague fumbled with the defibrillator, hands shaking as he tried to set it up.

"Someone call 911!" the employee doing CPR shouted.

Liz stepped forward, her face pale. "I already did. They're on their way."

"Call them again!" the employee snapped, not pausing in his compressions. "Tell them it's a Code Blue. We need someone, stat!"

Liz nodded frantically, pulling out her phone again. Her fingers trembled as she dialed, and I could see tears welling in her eyes. She walked out of the room.

The other employee finally got the defibrillator pads in place. "Clear!" he called out, and we all took a step back as Dominic's body jerked from the shock.

Renee let out a choked sob, burying her face in her hands. Jack stood frozen. The two of them stood together, and it was heartening to see him protectively place his hand on her back.

"Still no pulse," the first employee announced grimly. "Continuing CPR."

The room was a cacophony of sounds that echoed in the cavernous space: the rhythmic thuds of chest compressions, the mechanical voice of the defibrillator giving instructions, Liz's shaky tone as she updated the 911 dispatcher, Renee's muffled sobs, and Jack's ragged breathing.

The visions I'd seen felt important, but how did they connect to what was happening now? Then again, maybe they had nothing to do with his death.

People died of heart attacks all the time while exercising, right? Dominic had to be at least fifty, maybe even fifty-five. Prime age for men and vascular issues. Still, he seemed quite fit.

As the distant wail of sirens grew louder, I couldn't shake the feeling that whatever happened to Dominic Harper, it wasn't a simple medical issue.

An hour later, the pickleball court had transformed into an active investigation. The once pristine blue floor was now marred by sneaker scuff marks, discarded medical equipment, and Dominic's body, which was now mercifully covered in a white sheet.

I sat on the floor at the edge of the room, my back against the cool wall, everyone bustling around. My legs felt like jelly, and the adrenaline that had coursed through my body earlier had long since faded, leaving me feeling drained and exhausted.

Police officers milled about, their radios crackling with chatter. Forensic technicians in white coveralls meticulously photographed and collected evidence, their movements precise and slow.

Renee paced one wall. Liz was opposite me, talking on the phone. I think she was telling the entire town about what happened. My eyes went to the town's medical examiner, Dr. Heather Yates. I didn't know her personally, but I'd met her son, a local radio DJ who broadcasted to both humans and the spirit world. I almost wanted to introduce myself; she and Oliver had been on a couple of dates before I'd moved to town.

Now didn't seem like the time for a social chat, though. She was obviously busy.

Amidst the commotion, a tall, broad-shouldered man strode into the room, his presence snapping everyone to attention.

Police Chief Christopher Wolf had arrived.

Given my recent history with various incidents around town, I braced myself for a lecture. Chief Wolf was a good guy, but he also had been skeptical of my "poking around" in incidents over the past several months. The fact that I was even here when someone died would probably raise his hackles.

His piercing eyes scanned the room, taking in every detail with a cool, professional gaze. As he moved, officers instinctively stepped aside, their respect for him obvious with their deferential nods. I half expected them to salute.

"What's the situation?" Wolf barked, his deep voice bouncing around the room.

A young officer hurried over, notepad in hand. "Victim is Dominic Harper, sir. Fifty-three years old. Collapsed during a pickleball game approximately ninety minutes ago. CPR was attempted by both the facility and paramedics, but he was pronounced dead at the scene."

Wolf nodded, his jaw clenching. "Any signs of foul play?"

"Nothing obvious, sir, but the M.E. hasn't finished her preliminary examination yet. It's early enough in the day that they should be able to finish the autopsy by tomorrow morning. We also need to notify next of kin."

As Wolf continued to receive his briefing, his eyes darted from one person to the next, eventually landing on Liz, who had ended her call and was staring at him while sniffling.

His stern expression softened almost imperceptibly, a change I doubted anyone else would have noticed if they didn't know about their relationship.

Although, come to think of it, *everyone* knew about their relationship. This was Cypress Grove, where the only thing more common than the metaphysical goings-on was the town gossip.

"Officer Johnson," Wolf said, his tone softening slightly while motioning for a younger cop to approach, "please make sure that all witnesses are comfortable and have given their statements. Copy that?"

"Consider it done, sir," the officer replied, scurrying off.

Wolf made his way over to Liz, who was sitting on a nearby bench, looking pale and shaken.

I could see the conflict in his eyes. I suspected it was a professional need to maintain composure warring with his personal desire to give her a big hug.

"Hey," he said softly. "How are you holding up?"

Liz managed a weak smile. "I'm okay, Chris. But. Wow. This is a lot to process. Everything happened so fast. They tried to save him, but..."

Wolf nodded, his hands twitching at his side as if he wanted to reach out and embrace her — but couldn't because it would look unprofessional. "I understand. We'll need to get your statement, but take your time to gather yourself. Officer Johnson will be over shortly. Have you had any water?"

"I have." She sniffled, and he reached into his pocket for a pack of tissues. He handed her the entire thing.

"I need to lock down this scene. Hang tight, okay? I won't be far."

She nodded.

As he turned to walk away, Liz caught his arm. "Chris," she said softly. "Thank you."

For a moment, Wolf's professional facade cracked, and I saw the depth of his feelings for Liz in his eyes. He quickly caressed her arm before reluctantly letting go and returning to his duties.

I adored Liz, and the fact that she was dating a tender, kind person was a relief. Even if he did tend to talk in police dispatcher lingo. The man was wild about her.

The door to the court swung open, and more people from the medical examiner's office entered, pushing a gurney. As they prepared to move Dominic's body, a commotion erupted in the hallway.

"Let me through! I need to see him!"

A young woman burst onto the court, shoving aside a Pickled employee.

Her designer heels clacked against the floor. She was stunningly beautiful, with long, dark hair and piercing, near-black eyes that were now wide and wild. Her teal dress was pristine, yet her smokey eye makeup was smudged.

Renee, Liz, and I instinctively moved toward each other and huddled in the corner of the court.

"Ma'am, you can't be in here," an officer said, moving to intercept the young woman.

"I'm his assistant," she said in an icy tone. "Please, I need to see Dominic! Now."

Wolf strode over, his face set in a grim mask. "Miss, I'm Chief Christopher Wolf. I understand you're upset, but this is an active scene. We can't allow you to contaminate the area. We'll need you to take a seat in the hallway while our techs process everything. You copy?"

"A scene? A crime scene? What happened?" The woman's eyes darted around the room, finally landing on Dominic's body. Her face crumpled, and she let out a heart-wrenching wail. "Oh, Dom! No!"

As the officers tried to calm her down, her gaze locked onto the three of us. Her grief turned to fury in an instant.

"You!" she snarled, pointing. "You all did this! Dom told me he was playing against some witches today. What did you do to him?"

Renee gasped. "We didn't do anything! It was only a game!"

The woman lunged forward, her voice rising to a shriek. "Liars! You used your witchcraft on him! You killed Dom!"

Wolf and another officer grabbed her arms, holding her back as she struggled against them.

"Miss, calm down," the chief said firmly, almost ensuring that she wouldn't, in fact, calm down. In my experience, telling someone to calm down did the opposite. "We don't know what happened yet. Insults and theories won't help anyone, least of all our officers. For all we know, this was due to natural causes."

But the woman tried to wriggle away. "Test them!" she screamed. "Test them for magic! They killed him with their spells and potions and whatever stupid stuff they use! Dominic was in perfect health. He had a physical last week. Get his medical records! You'll see! This was murder!"

My jaw dropped. The woman's accusations were ridiculous. How did one "test" for magic and have it be admissible in a court of law? Was that a thing? Plus, I didn't have the foggiest idea of how to use magic to win a pickleball game, much less kill some-one. Why would we want to murder Dom in the first place?

And the same went for Renee and Liz. Although... Renee might have worked a spell on that ball. *Might* being the operative word. The knot in my stomach tightened. Perhaps it was best to keep that particular theory to myself.

Wolf managed to calm the woman, speaking to her in low, serious tones. As she calmed down, I saw her eyes narrow as they landed on our group again. There was calculation behind her grief now, a sharpness that made me uneasy.

"Chief Wolf," she said, her voice suddenly steady. "I want to file a formal complaint against these three women. I believe they're responsible for Dominic's death, and I have evidence to prove it. He told me he was playing against some witches. In fact, he texted me about a half hour ago and said they were cheating. And I have more evidence. Or I've heard about the evidence."

Wolf's eyebrows shot up. "Evidence? What kind of evidence?"

The woman straightened her jacket, composing herself. "Dominic kept a journal. He wrote about strange things happening at the gallery, things he couldn't explain. And he mentioned witchcraft to me. He's had issues ever since he opened the gallery in this cursed town."

My heart began to pound. What could Dominic have possibly written about witchcraft? Plus, there were dozens of witches in town. Hundreds, maybe. And how did Dominic's journal prove anything?

Wolf looked skeptical but professional. "We'll need to see this journal, Miss...?"

"Francis," she supplied. "Vanessa Francis. I'm not only Dom's assistant; I'm also his fiancée. I don't know where the journal is. Don't know where he kept it."

Jack, who had been quietly giving his statement to an officer, suddenly looked up, his face pale.

"Fiancée? I've never seen you before. Fiancee?" he repeated, his voice hoarse. The sound was so unnatural that everyone stopped what they were doing and stared at him. "Dom never mentioned..."

Vanessa's eyes locked onto Jack. "Who the eff are you?" she asked, her tone haughty.

Before Jack could answer, Wolf stepped in. "Ms. Francis, we'll need you to make a statement. Officer Johnson will assist with that, and we'll want to see that journal as soon as possible. Please talk to our officer in private."

As Vanessa was led away, Liz, Renee, and I turned to one another.

"What the heck?" Liz whispered.

"She's probably in shock, poor thing," Renee said.

"Weird," I whispered.

Wolf stood in the middle of the room. "Alright, everyone. We've got a lot to sort out here. No one leaves until they've given their statement. That means you three," he said, nodding to Liz, Renee, and me. "I'll need to speak with you each separately. The club has offered us use of a conference room. Ms. Matthews, I'll start with you first."

As I followed the chief out of the room and down the hall, an uncomfortable truth hit me.

This was the second untimely death I'd been involved with since coming to Cypress Grove ten months ago. What were the odds?

<h1 style="text-align:center">Six</h1>

Eight hours later, I wove my way through the crowds at the Neon Nights Street Fair. It was among one of the many festivals in Cypress Grove, and this one was held every Saturday evening in the summer months.

Unlike the majority of the street fairs in town, this one was a couple of miles from downtown, in a small village neighborhood with boutiques and shops.

I was running late. Tardiness used to be my norm, but somehow, I'd managed to get my act together in midlife. Well, usually. I'd had a hectic day, what with Dominic's death and then later, a ton of inn duties. I'd hoped to work in a nap, but that had been impossible because of my guests at the Crescent Moon.

Tonight, they were all at a magic show at the town's pavilion, and since they were repeat guests, I didn't feel the need to stay home this evening. As a relatively new inn owner, I was trying to find the balance between being an attentive host and hovering. Unexpectedly inheriting a business I knew nothing about had been a challenge. An interesting and exciting one, but occasionally it was fraught with indecision.

Still, I'd been looking forward to this street festival, mostly because it was my first night to staff the coven's booth. We sold jars of honey harvested by our members, and all of us took turns working the various festivals around town.

I was meeting Liz and another coven member here. As I hustled from my car to the booth in the park, I realized something else with a twinge of dread: this was also the neighborhood where Dominic's gallery was located. Several shops ringed the park: a cafe with sidewalk tables and hanging plants, a bar, a bookstore, and Dominic's gallery.

Since the streets around the park were closed to traffic, I dashed across when I spotted our booth. To my surprise, only Liz was there when I arrived.

"Hey," I said, a little breathless. "Why are you the only one here? Where's Jane?"

"Hi, I just got here myself. Jane did most of the setup, and then she had to run. Her dog is having tummy troubles, and I told her to go home and baby him. Oh, and I saw Oliver. He's here and is coming over in a while. Wanted me to tell you he's visiting a friend, some guy who runs a craft cocktail kit booth over there. He was delivering a large jug of water to his cocktail friend. I wanted to tell him about today but he was in a rush." She gestured to her left.

"Oh, cool. How are you feeling?"

"Physically, or emotionally?"

"Either. Both."

She took a fortifying inhale. "Physically, I'm okay. I took a non-narcotic pain pill and Ubered here. So I'm feeling pretty decent. Emotionally, I'm not so sure. Being questioned by one of your boyfriend's officers is never a fun experience."

"Being questioned by *your boyfriend* isn't a fun experience either." I paused, then worried that she would take offense. "I'm joking. Chris was actually quite nice and professional, as he always is. Today was so awful, wasn't it?"

"Sure was. I'm worried for Renee."

"Same. Have you heard from her?"

"She was still talking to the officers when I left, and that was around three. She was in there for hours."

A jolt of awareness went through me. I had talked with Chief Wolf, and then had been allowed to go after about twenty minutes. That was at about one in the afternoon. "I wonder why they kept her so long? I tried texting her a couple of hours ago but she didn't respond."

"She didn't return my calls. I don't get a good feeling."

"Are you saying that in a general way, or in some sort of clairvoyant way?"

"I'm not sure. That's the issue. My intuition is fuzzy."

Until recently, Liz hadn't experienced any psychic, metaphysical, or other abilities. She was a practicing witch, but unlike me, she didn't have a specific power. I suspected this bothered her; however, she had been taking spell work classes and appeared to be honing her skills in that department. I was learning that some people (like me) had inherent powers. Others had to learn and sharpen their innate ability.

She glanced over my shoulder. "Look at that. Dominic's gallery is open tonight. Wowzers. That takes some guts."

I turned to follow Liz's gaze, my eyes landing on Dominic's building. The lights were on inside, casting a bright glow onto the sidewalk. People spilled out, laughing and drinking wine.

It seemed oddly out of place, considering the day's events.

"Whoa. Yikes. You're right," I said, frowning. "That is strange. You'd think they'd close up shop, at least for tonight. You'd think the cops would make them shut down."

Liz leaned in closer, her voice dropping to a whisper. "I heard some things about Dominic from a Realtor friend. Apparently, he wasn't only dealing in art."

My eyebrows shot up. "What do you mean?"

She glanced around before continuing. "My neighbor heard rumors that he was involved in some shady business dealings. Nothing concrete, but people were speculating about money laundering through the gallery."

Dominic seemed like the kind of guy to launder money, but was that my bias showing? "That's quite an accusation. Do you think it's true?"

Liz lifted a shoulder. "My neighbor tends to get carried away with gossip, so who knows? She was totally wrong when she thought another of our neighbors was amassing a reptile army."

I let out a nervous laugh, unsure if she was being serious.

My laughter faded as we continued to study the gallery. The front window displayed a collection of abstract paintings in shades of red and black. It looked like blood to me, and I shuddered.

"Why do you think they're open?" I mused. "Surely they'd want to close out of respect, or at least to deal with everything."

Liz shrugged. "Maybe they're trying to maintain a sense of normalcy? Or maybe they have an artist who was scheduled to attend and they didn't want to cancel? Who knows."

Before I could respond, we were interrupted by a woman bursting through the passing crowd. It was Zoe Gevalt, a young reporter from the local paper, practically sprinting towards us. Her cheeks were flushed, and she was slightly out of breath when she reached our booth.

"Amelia! Liz!" she panted, her eyes wide with excitement. "I'm so glad I found you, because you'll never believe what I just heard!"

I exchanged a quick glance with Liz before turning back to Zoe. "What? And hi. Long time no see. What's it been, six hours?"

She had cornered me several hours ago in the parking lot of Pickled shortly after I'd given my statement to the police, eager for any details about Dominic's collapse. She'd heard the police traffic on her scanner. I'd been careful when talking with her, sticking to the facts and avoiding speculation.

"Hi." Zoe lowered her voice conspiratorially. "I got word from my sources at the police department. The preliminary autopsy results are in. Not the toxicology tests, those take a while. They're saying Dominic was murdered!"

I gripped the edge of our booth, steadying myself. "Murdered? Are you sure? It seemed more like a heart attack or a stroke or something physical. He dropped to the floor."

Zoe nodded vigorously. "My source is reliable. They found evidence of poison in his system. It wasn't natural causes like everyone thought."

As this news sank in, I thought of the vision I'd had earlier. The argument, the anger, the raw emotion. Had I witnessed a prelude to murder? And if so, who was responsible?

Or had it been a scene from Dominic's sketchy past? Nothing made sense.

I looked back at the gallery. What was going on in there? The fact that they were open when the owner had been *murdered* only hours ago seemed extra ghoulish.

"Have you been in the gallery?" Liz asked.

Zoe groaned. "I have, but was immediately kicked out since I'd done a story on the place when it opened and someone recognized me. They said no reporters, but they're in there having cocktails and appetizers."

"Really," Liz said slowly, her voice filled with interest.

"Yeah. Can I interview you now? I know you declined earlier today, but thought I'd ask you again."

"Zoe, I'd love to talk with you about all this, but since I'm dating the chief, it's probably for the best that I don't comment. You understand, right?" Liz gave her an apologetic smile.

Zoe nodded, looking a bit disappointed. "Of course, I get it. Well, I've got to run and update my article with these new details. I saw you from across the street and figured you'd want to know the latest. See ya!" With that, she dashed off, her notebook clutched tightly to her chest.

As we watched her disappear into the crowd, I turned to Liz. "Do you think we should—"

But before I could finish my thought, two middle-aged women approached our booth, their eyes bright with curiosity.

"Excuse me," one of them said, her gaze falling on the jars of honey displayed before us. "Is this the midlife coven?"

I plastered on my best welcoming smile, pushing thoughts of murder and poison to the back of my mind. "Hello! Yes, this is the Sisters of Hecate booth. We're a coven for Gen X women. I'd love to tell you more about our group."

The second woman nodded eagerly. "Oh yes! We recently moved to Cypress Grove, and heard so much about the magical community here. Do you offer memberships?"

Liz and I exchanged a quick glance, silently agreeing to put our discussion about Dominic's death on hold. We had a job to do, after all.

"We absolutely offer memberships," Liz cooed. "Let me tell you about some of the benefits of joining our organization."

As she launched into her well-practiced spiel about monthly meetings, workshops, and community service projects, I found my mind wandering back to the gallery across the street. The laughter and tinkling of glasses drifting from its open doors seemed more sinister now, knowing that I'd witnessed the owner's final moments.

I forced myself to focus on the potential new coven members, nodding along as Liz explained our upcoming full moon ritual and honey harvest.

The two women signed up for the coven's newsletter, bought two jars of honey, and took brochures. When Liz and I were finally alone again, I turned to her.

"I feel like going to the gallery to poke around."

Liz stared at me with wild eyes. "Me too."

"But we can't leave the booth."

"No. We shouldn't."

As Liz and I exchanged looks of frustration, a familiar figure caught my eye, approaching our booth with an easy, sexy stride. I felt a fizz of excitement when I recognized the man.

Oliver Everhart.

"Well, hello there, ladies," Oliver said, his deep voice sending a pleasant shiver down my spine. He leaned in, pressing a soft kiss to my cheek before flashing us both that wickedly charming smile of his. "How was your day?"

I hesitated, realizing I hadn't updated him on the terrible events. He'd been teaching summer classes on the paranormal history of Florida at the college in Orlando, and I'd planned on telling him about Dominic later, in private, in person. It didn't seem like the kind thing to explain in a random text message.

Before I could come up with a logical response, Liz jumped in. "Oh, you know, the usual in Cypress Grove. The man who owns that gallery across the street was murdered right in front of us, Amelia was stabbed, and Renee was questioned by the police for a long time."

"I was not stabbed," I retorted. "Well, not intentionally."

Oliver's smile faltered, his eyebrows shooting up in surprise. He rubbed the back of his neck, a gesture I'd come to recognize as his way of processing unexpected information. "I remember a time when I knew if people were joking, or telling a strange but true story. Today is not that time."

I shot Liz an exasperated look, but she seemed unfazed. Instead, she turned to Oliver with a mischievous glint in her eye. "Will you man the booth while we go to the gallery to snoop around?"

"Liz!" I exclaimed, mortified by her bluntness. But part of me was a little jealous that I didn't come up with the idea.

Oliver looked between us, his expression a mix of concern and amusement. "I think," he said slowly, "that I'm going to need a bit more information before I agree to anything. Amelia, babe, care to fill me in on what exactly happened today?"

I gave him the quick, just-the-facts details.

"So basically, Dominic — the owner of that gallery there — collapsed during our pickleball game," I began.

Liz chimed in, "And then he had the audacity to die right

there mid-game, when it was basically tied. Talk about poor sportsmanship."

Oliver's eyes widened, and Liz immediately backpedaled. "Sorry, that was in poor taste. Gallows humor is my coping mechanism."

I continued, "Anyway, we'd like to check out the gallery. Something seems off about them being open tonight."

Oliver sighed, running a hand through his hair. "It's probably not a good idea for you two to go snooping around a potential crime scene," he paused, a wry smile tugging at his lips, "but when has that ever stopped you?"

Liz and I exchanged excited glances. "So, you'll watch the booth?" I asked hopefully.

"Be careful, okay? Don't get arrested. Uh, and what am I selling here?"

"Honey," I said.

"Yeah?" Oliver responded.

"No. Honey." I picked up a jar.

"It's easy," Liz said. "Here's the price list, and here's the cash box. And hand out brochures for the coven to anyone who looks like they're between the ages of 44 and 59."

"That seems oddly specific," he mumbled, lifting a jar to his face and squinting at the label. "Should I card people?"

"Thanks." I brushed my mouth over his cheek. As usual, he smelled like soap, spice, and man. It was a romance novel cliché, but the man smell on Oliver was extremely alluring. "We'll be back in a flash."

With that, Liz and I dashed out of the park across the street, blending into the crowd as we approached the gallery. As we entered, we tried our best to look casual.

"Oh, look at this abstract piece," Liz exclaimed in an exaggerated posh accent as we paused at a painting that might have been a woman, but also could have been a wrench.

I played along. "The artist's use of color is simply divine."

A waiter approached with drinks on a tray. I took one that

was fizzy and looked like champagne. Liz extended her arm before I gently reminded her, "Uh, Liz? Your medication?"

"I'm not taking any pain meds, but still. You're probably right," she sighed, withdrawing her hand. "No bubbly for me."

The waiter, overhearing, offered, "We have a delicious non-alcoholic mocktail if you'd prefer, ma'am."

Liz fluttered her eyelashes at him. "That would be perfect, thank you."

He gestured toward a milky blue concoction, also in a champagne flute. Liz took one and sipped.

"Raspberry," she said. "Not bad."

As we huddled in a corner, I turned to her. "Are you seeing what I'm seeing? It's like nothing happened. The owner died hours ago, and they're throwing a party."

Liz nodded, her eyes narrowing as she scanned the room. "It's surreal. Either they're in serious denial, or something very strange is going on here. Oh, crap. There's Dominic's assistant, the one from today. The one who has it in for witches. Pretend like we're admiring the art behind us."

She quickly turned so her back was facing the room and began gesturing as if she was making an important point. To anyone else, it would appear that we were especially interested in... the wall thermostat.

"We probably should have thought this out a little more," I muttered while trying to sneak a side glance to see where Vanessa was.

"Yeah, we kinda neglected to consider what would happen if we saw her. Our bad."

"I didn't think she'd be here since her fiancé died a few hours ago. She's walking down a hall, now out of sight," I whispered. "Probably our cue to leave."

"Heck, no. C'mon."

I hesitated, but Liz grabbed my arm and pulled me deeper into the gallery. It was rather maze-like, with walls and makeshift panels showcasing the art. As we rounded a corner, we nearly ran into an older man. A familiar older man.

"Jack!" I exclaimed, almost spilling my champagne. "What are you doing here?"

Before he could answer, a waiter materialized beside us, balancing a tray of impossibly tiny appetizers.

"Canapé, anyone?" he offered politely. "We have mini spanakopita, and gold leaf-dusted vegan chocolate bonbons."

Liz and I exchanged glances, our eyebrows raised. Despite the absurdity of the situation, my stomach growled. I realized the only thing I'd eaten were two cookies at home and a granola bar in my purse while at the pickleball club.

"You know what? I'll try the spinach puff pastry." I reached for the good-sized morsel. "Heck, I'll take two."

Liz shrugged. "When in Rome. I'll have the vegan bonbon."

We popped the bites into our mouths. Well, yum. It was an express train to Flavortown. Rich, salty, and definitely satisfying. I could easily eat a dinner portion.

"Geez," Liz mumbled, her eyes widening. "That's actually really tasty."

I nodded in agreement with a full mouth, already eyeing the remaining snacks on the tray.

Jack chuckled at our reactions. "Careful, ladies. Those things are addictive. And about three hundred calories each, if I had to guess."

I snorted and reached for a third. "Like we care."

The waiter, maintaining his professional demeanor, offered the tray to Jack when I was finished. "And for you, sir?"

"Thank you, but I'm afraid I've already indulged a little too much tonight."

The waiter moved on, and I was beginning to like Jack a little less. Any man who tried to shame women over calories was sketchy, at least in my book.

"Well," Jack said, "now that you've had your gourmet snack, let's find somewhere quiet to talk."

He turned to walk down the hall. Liz and I exchanged excited looks.

We followed him into a smaller room, away from the main gallery space. A couple was peering at a canvas on one wall.

The pieces in here were smaller, more intimate, mostly landscapes. At least I think they were landscapes. Jack, who was holding a bottle of Perrier, took a long sip. His amused expression was gone, and in the brighter light of this room, I could see the dark circles under his red eyes.

"This is a lot to handle. I came here thinking I'd find Dom's family, but when I arrived, there was all this." He gestured toward the main room. "I'm blown away. Why would Vanessa do this?"

Liz nodded. "We were thinking the same thing. It seems disrespectful, at the very least."

Jack ran a hand through his silver hair, his brow furrowed. "How's Renee doing? I've been worried about her. After my interview, cops told me to leave, but she was still there, being questioned. This whole situation must be so stressful."

"We haven't talked with her since this morning either," I said. "But yeah, the police had quite a few questions for her."

Jack's eyes widened. "Really? Why? I mean, it was clearly some kind of medical issue, right?"

I hesitated, unsure how much to reveal. Liz, always the direct one, jumped in feet first. "Actually, we heard it might not have been natural causes after all. *Homicide.*"

Jack nearly choked on his champagne. "What? But that's... that's impossible. We were all with him."

"We heard from a local reporter that he was poisoned," Liz whispered loudly.

"Wow. I would've never thought... Unless..." He trailed off, his gaze distant.

"Unless what?" I prodded.

Jack leaned in close, his voice dropping to a whisper. "Look, I probably shouldn't say anything, but Dom was acting strange lately. Paranoid. I've only known him for a few months but he's changed over the last few weeks."

I felt a little jolt of excitement. Did Chief Wolf know about this? "Did you tell the cops this?"

Jack shook his head. "I didn't think it was significant, but now that I see all this, here, maybe there's something with that Vanessa woman. She seems odd, doesn't she?"

Liz and I nodded enthusiastically.

"Dom never mentioned her?" Liz asked.

"Nope. We were mostly gym buddies. We never talked about women. You know what? I'll call the police and tell them about his paranoia."

"Was he paranoid about anything specific?"

Jack made a face. "That someone was going to curse him or something. It sounded pretty out there and I always changed the subject because it sounded too weird and embarrassing. I didn't mention it to the cops this afternoon because I assumed he died from a medical thing. Crap, I'm a fool. What time is it?"

He checked his phone. "It's only eight-thirty. I'll make that call now. The detective gave me his card."

"Good idea," Liz said, her eyes darting around the nearly empty room.

Jack's gaze ping-ponged between the two of us. "If you talk with Renee, please let her know I'm thinking of her, okay? She's a real special lady, and I'd like to get to know her better."

"Will do," I said.

"Sure," chimed in Liz, whose attention seemed distracted.

Jack squeezed both of us on our upper arms and left.

I watched him walk out and turned to Liz. Something about Jack was odd. "He's kinda—"

"Look. There's a door over there." She gestured with her mocktail glass. "What do you think is behind it?"

"I dunno. A closet, maybe? Why?"

As the couple wandered out of the room, her eyes sparkled

with mischief. "This is our chance," she whispered, nodding towards the door. "No one's around. Let's check it out."

55

with mischief. "This is our chance," she whispered, nodding towards the door. "No one's around. Let's check it out."

Seven

"Liz, I don't think—"

"Oh, come on, we're already here," she interrupted, grabbing my arm. "If anyone catches us, we'll say we're looking for the bathroom. Easy peasy, lemon squeezy."

I sighed. When Liz got an idea in her head, there was no stopping her. "Fine, but if we get arrested, you're paying the bail money. And you're explaining everything to the police chief. Your boyfriend."

"Let me handle all that. Don't you worry."

As I was hesitating, I heard a woman's loud voice in the hall. "Yes, it's so upsetting about Dominic. Thank you for coming. I appreciate you so much. I'm devastated."

"I think that's Vanessa," Liz hissed, pulling me along. "Let's go."

"She doesn't sound devastated," I muttered.

We hustled towards the door, trying our best to look casual, but probably failing miserably. It was a nondescript white door, almost blending into the wall. The kind of door you'd walk right past without a second glance. A silver handle gleamed in the overhead can lights.

"It's probably a storage closet," I said, more to convince

myself than Liz. "We'll open it and find a bunch of supplies and maybe a mop. They must have to clean a lot to keep a place looking this spotless."

Liz ignored me and turned the handle. She yanked the door open. Surprisingly, it was unlocked.

My jaw dropped. Instead of brooms and buckets, we were staring into a large, dark space.

"Quick," Liz hissed, shoving me inside. "Before someone sees us!"

We stumbled into the room, and Liz quietly closed the door behind us. It was now pitch black.

"Well," I whispered to Liz, my heart pounding, "we're in. Now what?"

"We need some light," Liz whispered, fumbling along the wall and crashing into me in the process. "There's gotta be a switch somewhere."

I grabbed her arm, hissing, "No! We can't risk someone noticing a light suddenly coming on in here. Use your phone."

There was a muffled thud and a soft curse from Liz. "Dropped it."

I sighed, fishing my own phone out of my jeans pocket, and managed to activate the flashlight feature. A beam of light cut through the darkness.

"Oh whoa," I said. Liz scrambled to pick up her phone and turned on her flashlight.

We were surrounded by canvases. Most were covered with cloth drapes, but a few stood exposed, leaning against three walls. There were dozens of them, all different shapes and sizes. Stacked three, four, five deep. As I shone the light around, I noticed something odd.

The room smelled of dust, and Liz sneezed into the crook of her arm. She had the most delicate sneeze, like a kitten. "Allergies," she said. "*Choo.*"

"Liz," I whispered, "look at these paintings. They're old and not abstract."

Liz walked to one stack and lifted a drape. It was a still life of fruit.

"This is familiar," she said. "And famous."

"Really? Don't all still lifes with fruit look the same?"

I peeked under a cloth. It was a Renaissance-looking portrait. While I knew zero about art, I knew these were nothing like the modern pieces displayed in the gallery. The paintings in here were classical in style, with rich colors and ornate frames, not sleek black borders.

I took a deep breath, steeling myself. "Liz, I'm going to see if I can pick up any visions."

Liz's playful demeanor vanished instantly. She knew the toll these visions could take on me — headaches, vertigo, even fainting. With a solemn nod, she whispered, "I'm right here in case you need help."

With my phone in my left hand, I approached the nearest painting, its ornate frame glinting in the beam of my phone's flashlight. Gingerly, I ran the fingers of my right hand along the gilded edge. The world shifted, and suddenly I was transported to a dusty workshop. A bearded man lovingly carved intricate details into the wood, his calloused hands moving with surprising grace.

I blinked, returning to the present. Sometimes that's all I got, mundane glimpses into an object's past. Nothing earth-shattering, merely snippets of everyday life. Truthfully, that was the coolest part of my psychometry, seeing people from the past doing regular things.

Undeterred, I moved from frame to frame, touching each one briefly. Most yielded similar results: fleeting images of craftsmen, art dealers, or gallery workers. Nothing that screamed "clue" about Dominic's death or whatever secrets this room held.

Finally, I hesitated before an uncovered painting. It depicted a woman with flowing golden hair and a serene expression, draped in sumptuous robes against a backdrop of shells and flowers.

"I think that's a Botticelli," Liz whispered, her eyes wide with awe.

I turned to her, eyebrow raised. "Really? You possess all sorts of arcane knowledge, you know that?"

She shrugged. "I went to Italy with my ex-husband about a decade ago when we were trying to save our marriage. We did a weeklong class at some big museum. Botticelli was the mack daddy of the Renaissance painters."

"Well, that means you're the expert in this room, because my idea of great art is Bob Ross," I joked, and she snickered softly.

I turned back to the painting, my hand hovering over its surface. With a shake of my head, I pressed my palm lightly against the canvas. It felt weird to touch such an old painting, and I tried to only have contact with a small patch at the bottom.

The rough texture of the acrylics felt unfamiliar under my fingers.

Then the world around me vanished in an instant, replaced by a scene so vivid and intense it nearly knocked me off my feet. I was in a dimly lit room, smoke hanging thick in the air. Dominic stood there, his face flushed with anger, gesturing wildly at a man I didn't recognize.

"You promised me top quality fakes!" Dominic hissed. "These won't fool anyone who even has a semester in art history!"

The other man, a stocky figure with a scar across his cheek, sneered. "You're getting what you paid for, Harper. If you want better, it'll cost you. Next time, take it up with your connection. I don't have time to deal with you."

"Cost me?" Dominic scoffed. "I'm already in deep with your organization. How much more do you vultures want?"

A third man, lurking in the shadows, spoke up. His voice was calm, but it sent chills down my spine. "Mr. Harper, perhaps you've forgotten the nature of our arrangement. We own you now. You'll take what we give you and be grateful. All of these have impeccable provenance paperwork."

The vision swirled, showing me flashes of other scenes, like a montage in a movie. Men in expensive suits exchanging briefcases.

Paintings being carefully packed and shipped. Money changing hands in dark places.

It looked like I was witnessing something far bigger than a shady art deal. This was an organized criminal network, and Dominic was part of it.

When I thought I couldn't take any more, the vision began to fade. But not before I caught one last glimpse of Dominic's face, twisted with fear. He was sweating. Far more than he had while playing pickleball.

I gasped as I snapped back to reality, stumbling backward. Liz steadied me before I could fall.

"Amelia? What did you see?"

I opened my mouth to respond, but before I could utter a sound, the door to the storage room swung open. Light flooded in, momentarily blinding me. As my eyes adjusted, I found myself staring into what looked like the barrel of a gun.

"Well, well," a familiar voice drawled. "What do we have here?"

Liz threw her arms around me and yelled, "Oh my goddess!" She then sneezed into my shoulder.

I grabbed her into a protective hug and let out a scream that sounded more like an injured seagull choking on a particularly large French fry. "Don't shoot!"

"Well. That was embarrassing."

Liz and I sat in plush leather chairs in what appeared to be someone's office. Possibly Dominic's, but it was too bland to determine who really worked in here.

The room was lit by only a small desk lamp casting shadows across framed certificates and awards on the walls. The air smelled of leather and expensive cologne, a contrast to the musty scent of the storage room we'd been caught snooping in.

"I can't believe Chris caught us," Liz groaned, burying her

face in her hands. "Of all the people who could've found us, it had to be my boyfriend. Well, we had a good run, I guess. I found the one decent single man in town and I had to screw it up."

I sighed, still feeling the sting of shame. "At least it wasn't actually a gun. Though I'm not sure Chris's flashlight was much better, considering how he aimed it right in our faces. Then marching us out of that room like common criminals."

"Don't remind me." Liz peeked at me through her fingers. "Did you see all those people staring while Chris and that other officer paraded us through the gallery? I swear I saw Mrs. Winslow taking notes. This'll be all over town tomorrow."

I grimaced, remembering the sea of shocked faces as we'd been escorted out of the storage room. The party had gone eerily quiet, all eyes on us as we'd been led out of the storage room. (Fortunately, not in handcuffs). "Maybe they'll think we're art thieves. It could add to my mysterious newcomer reputation."

Liz snorted, dropping her hands. "Yeah, right."

We sat in silence for a moment, the gravity of our absurd situation sinking in.

"Liz," I said slowly, "do you think we're going to be arrested? Should I call Oliver?"

I groaned. He'd almost certainly come here if I texted him, but we couldn't leave the booth empty, and even if he somehow packed it up, well, that would mean the coven would lose out on honey sales. I didn't want him to worry. Probably best to leave him there, for now. Unless we were really under arrest, of course.

She bit her lip, considering. "I don't know. I mean, we were trespassing, sort of. But it's not like we broke in."

"True," I nodded, "but we definitely weren't supposed to be in there. And after what I saw..." I trailed off, remembering the vision I'd had before we were caught.

Liz leaned forward, her eyes wide. "That's right! You never got to tell me what you saw."

As I explained everything, Liz's gaze swept over the desk. She picked up a pen. Then looked in a container and extracted a paperclip. Then she started going through the drawers of the desk.

I interrupted my story. "What are you doing?"

"Poking around. If Chris is going to break up with me and maybe arrest me, I might as well satisfy my curiosity."

"Hmm," I said, then continued telling her about my vision. When I was finished, half of Liz's arm was deep into a drawer. "Holy crap, Amelia. That's some serious stuff. We need to tell Chris about this."

"Yeah, but there are several flaws in that plan. One, we'd be admitting to almost breaking and entering."

"It was unlocked."

"True. But also, your boyfriend isn't exactly a believer of magic. Psychometric visions aren't admissible in court—"

I was cut off by the sound of wood scraping against wood. Liz had both arms in the drawer and was hunched over.

"What are you doing?" I hissed.

"Can you shine your cellphone light in here?" she whispered back.

I leaned over, trying to angle my phone's flashlight into the drawer without blocking Liz's rummaging hands. The awkward position had me half-standing, half-crouching.

"Ow." My arm started to cramp, and I contorted myself further, twisting my torso and stretching my neck to peer into the drawer alongside Liz.

"If we're going down for this, we might as well make it count. I've found a secret compartment. Uh-huh. Oh yeah. I'll bet the cops never even saw this."

I was about to protest when Liz suddenly froze. "Oh my goddess," she breathed, pulling out a black, leather-bound notebook. The pricey minimalist kind. "Check this out."

"What is it?"

"It might be the journal Vanessa mentioned earlier," Liz said, her voice barely above a whisper. "You know, the one where

Dominic supposedly wrote about witchcraft and strange happenings?"

I rubbed my cramped arm. "Open it. Quick!"

Liz flipped the cover open, her eyes scanning the first page. "It has dated entries."

Just as she was about to read further, we heard a familiar deep voice in the hallway.

Chief Wolf.

"Crap!" I whispered urgently. "What do we do?"

Panic flashed across Liz's face. She thrust the notebook towards me. "Here, take it!"

"What? No! You take it!" I shoved it back at her. "I don't even have a purse."

We went back and forth like this for a few seconds, locked in an absurd game of hot potato with potential evidence in a murder case.

Meanwhile, we could hear the chief's voice outside. "...why the hell did they continue with the party? We told them specifically not to open tonight. I don't understand."

The door handle began to turn.

"Fine." Liz shoved the notebook into her tie-dye hippie satchel right as the door swung open. Chief Wolf stood in the doorway, assessing us.

"Ladies," he said, his voice stern. "I think we need to have a serious talk about boundaries and interfering with an active investigation. The two of you can't go around acting like you're in a remake of I Love Lucy."

Why not, I wanted to joke. But didn't, because the chief had closed the door behind him and had launched into a lecture. A totally appropriate one, in my view. He obviously thought this was A Big Deal.

And it *was* a big deal. After all, we had stolen some possibly key evidence. In my humble opinion, I'd crossed several lines.

"We were only trying to find the bathroom," Liz said.

"Yeah, and then when we saw all the art, we thought we'd take a peek," I added.

Wolf looked at me, then at Liz. He sighed deeply. He closed his eyes and pinched the bridge of his nose. The sound of a clock ticking in the background somehow magnified his disappointment.

His shoulders sagged and he opened his eyes. "Look, I'm not going to arrest you two. The door was unlocked, and this is a public event. Technically, you didn't break any laws."

I felt a wave of relief wash over me, but it was short-lived as the chief's piercing gaze locked onto us.

"That being said, I need to know if you found anything in that room. Anything at all that might be relevant to our investigation."

I glanced at Liz, my mind racing. Should I tell him about my vision? About the paintings?

About the book that we'd pilfered?

Before I could decide, I blurted nervously, "Well, actually, Chief, I had a vision when I touched one of the paintings. I saw—"

"Stop right there, Amelia." Wolf held up a beefy hand. His expression was a mix of exasperation and disbelief. "We've been through this before. I can't base an investigation on your visions. I need concrete evidence, not supernatural hunches. I'm already up to my butt in alligators here. I'd told Vanessa not to open tonight because my officers were coming to look for evidence, and she opened anyway. This whole situation is a mess, from top to bottom."

I closed my mouth, feeling a twinge of frustration and fascination. Why had Vanessa so flagrantly ignored the authorities' request? Liz squeezed my arm sympathetically.

"Vanessa has agreed not to press charges for trespassing, but she was quite clear about one thing: neither of you are ever to set foot in this gallery again. Is that understood?"

We both nodded solemnly.

"Good," he said, his tone softening. He turned to Liz, his expression changing to one of concern. "Liz, sweetie, should you even be out right now? It's only been a few weeks since your surgery."

Liz smiled sheepishly. "I'm feeling much better, Chris. Really."

Wolf shook his head, a mix of affection and worry in his eyes. "Alright, but I'm getting one of my guys to take you home. You need rest. You don't need to gallivant around town."

"Amelia," he continued, turning back to me, "you're free to go. And please, try to stay out of trouble. At least for the rest of the night."

I nodded quickly and stood up, feeling both relieved and slightly guilty. "Um, thank you, Chief. We're really sorry about all this."

As I reached for the door handle, I glanced back at Liz. She gave me a small, reassuring smile, but I couldn't help wondering what she was going to do about the notebook hidden in her bag. And more importantly, what secrets it might contain about Dominic and his sketchy past.

I'd let Liz handle that for now. After all, the chief was *her* boyfriend and the book was in *her* bag.

I left the office, my mind reeling. As I stepped into the main gallery, I felt like I was walking through molasses. The air seemed to thicken and still around me. Every head in the room swiveled in my direction.

Gah. Embarrassing. Awkward. Fortunately, I didn't recognize anyone in here.

The partygoers, who moments ago had been chattering over cocktails and canapés, fell into silence. Their stares bore into me as I made my way through the room. I felt like a contestant in some bizarre beauty pageant, except instead of a tiara and sash, I was sporting a guilty conscience and the lingering scent of (possibly) forged art.

Probably body odor, too. I highly doubted my crayon-scented natural deodorant had withstood the events of the evening.

A woman in a sequined dress actually clutched her pearls as I passed. I half expected someone to faint dramatically or for a record to scratch to a halt.

I tried to maintain my dignity, chin up, shoulders back, channeling my inner Jackie O. But my feet had other ideas. As I neared the exit, I stumbled over my own feet, nearly face-planting into a waiter's tray of champagne flutes.

"Excuse me," I mumbled, my cheeks burning hotter than a Florida sidewalk in August.

A few people snickered. Jerks.

I finally made it to the door and ran smack into an invisible wall of humid night air. I instantly started to perspire.

I rushed back across the street to Oliver and our booth. He was dutifully explaining the merits of wildflower honey to an elderly couple.

As I approached, he looked up, relief washing over his face. "There you are!"

I smiled and stood behind the table alongside Oliver, helping bag the couple's honey purchase.

Once they'd left, Oliver turned and folded me into a hug. "I've sold a dozen bottles of honey. People really like this stuff. What do you say we give it all up and become beekeepers? We can go on the festival circuit. Seems to be pretty lucrative."

I snickered into his chest. "Sounds good to me."

He kissed the top of my head. "What happened in the gallery? I saw a police car pull up and the chief go in."

I grimaced. Dang, his arms around me felt good. Comforting. I didn't even care whether I smelled like crayon or B.O. or my sweet iris and vanilla perfume.

"Well, we didn't get arrested. For now, at least."

Eight

The next day, I hummed softly as I fluffed the pillows on the king-sized bed, enjoying the rare quiet morning at The Crescent Moon Inn. All our guests had left at the crack of dawn, eager to squeeze every last drop of magic out of their theme park tickets. Can't say I blamed them. Those things cost an arm, a leg, and probably a pint of blood these days.

Windex and microfiber cloth in hand, I moved on to the windows. The Florida sun streamed through the gauzy curtains, warming the room and highlighting the swirls of dust motes in the air. I made a mental note to give the drapes a good shake later.

As I worked, I thought about my own daughter, Jenny. When she was small, my ex and I had taken her to Disneyland in California. She'd been so excited to see Goofy, and I smiled thinking about that trip and how the three of us seemed to exist in one, perfect moment.

Jenny. My little girl, all grown up. She was now twenty-one and was coming for a visit next month. Even though I'd been in Cypress Grove for nearly ten months, she hadn't visited Florida yet — I'd flown to visit her during that time.

I told myself that it was easier that way, but part of me

wondered if I was reluctant to share my new world with her. Specifically, my psychometric powers and my witchy activities. Jenny didn't know her mom had joined a coven, talked to spirits, or solved mysteries.

When and how I'd tell Jenny all this was the real mystery in my life. The news was too big to send in a text, too complicated to capture in an email. I'd have preferred to call her on the phone, but since she was a Gen Z girl who rarely answered when an actual human was on the line, that was out of the question.

Speaking of, my phone was buzzing. I set down the Windex and reached in the back pocket of my cargo pants. It was a text from Liz, in all caps.

CAN YOU COME TO THE STORE TO
DISCUSS THE INVESTIGATION?

I frowned and tapped a response. Normally I went to Oliver's on Sundays for brunch. Today, however, he was at an event at his parents' church, so I was free. Sort of. A mountain of cleaning awaited here at the inn.

But there was no time to procrastinate like the present.

Sure. When? And why all caps?

We're in a serious situation. Come ASAP.

"What the duck?" I whispered aloud, employing my signature catchphrase that I'd used for years when I hadn't wanted to use the F-word around my young daughter.

OK, be there in an hour or less

I looked up. "Freddie!"

My giant orange cat, Freddie Purrcury, was on the freshly-made bed, nestling into the down duvet. He stretched out, obviously ready for a nap.

"You little stinker. When did you escape?" Freddie normally stayed downstairs in the apartment where I lived. Occasionally he crept out, much to the delight of my guests. (I made sure everyone who booked a room knew a cat was in the house in case of allergies).

"C'mon." I beckoned him.

He shut his eyes.

"No way, dude. I don't want to come back up here and clean up your furballs again."

I scooped him up and we trooped downstairs, him meowing in protest the entire way. A dried fish treat soothed his hurt feelings.

After showering, I changed into a breezy floral sundress and slipped on my most comfortable pair of sneakers.

I locked up the inn and set off towards downtown Cypress Grove. It was hotter than heck, but the thought of trying to find a parking spot on a Sunday morning was too daunting. Plus, most of the walk was shady, from the tall live oak trees.

Still, within a few steps, I could already feel beads of sweat forming at my temples.

As I neared Main Street, the faint scent of vanilla wafted through the air. On a whim, I ducked into Pangea, a local bakery, and bought a half-dozen assorted donuts.

Armed with a pink box of sugary goodness, I continued my trek to Liz's shop, The Astral Attic. As I approached, I noticed the 'CLOSED' sign hanging in the window. My heart rate kicked up a notch. Liz never closed on a Sunday because it was prime tourist shopping hours, so this must be serious indeed.

I knocked on the door, shifting the donut box to my hip. After a moment, I heard the click of a lock, and Liz's face appeared, her usually cheerful expression tinged with worry.

"Oh, Amelia, thank the goddess you're here," she said, ushering me inside. "And you brought donuts! You are truly a team player, lady."

The shop's interior was cool and dim, a welcome respite from the sweltering heat outside. In the background, soft pan flute music played. Liz had lit candles, even.

"I made some tea," Liz said, leading me towards the back. "Chamomile and lavender, with rooibos. Thought we could use something soothing."

"Sounds perfect," I replied, then paused. "Is Renee here yet?"

Liz nodded. "She's already in The Lounge."

As we rounded a corner, I caught sight of the shop's reading nook that Liz had dubbed "The Lounge." Plush armchairs and an overstuffed loveseat surrounded a low coffee table, all bathed in the soft glow of salt lamps. Renee sat perched on the edge of one chair, her fingers drumming an anxious rhythm on her knee.

Her face looked blotchy, either from the sun or crying. Could be either.

"Hey there," I called out softly, holding up the pink box. "I come bearing gifts of the frosted and sprinkled variety."

Renee's tense expression softened slightly. "Oh, you're incredible. I stress-ate my way through breakfast, but I'm already hungry again."

I set the box on the table. "I'm going to use the bathroom first. I'm a mess after that walk."

"You walked?" Renee glanced at me as if I'd lost my marbles.

"I know. I know. Amateur move. I'll be right back."

I went to the back of the store, where Renee was adding ice to a pitcher. "Making a pit stop," I said. "Be right there."

On the door of the bathroom was a new sign.

DUE TO RECENT EVENTS OUIJA BOARDS ARE
NO LONGER PERMITTED IN THE RESTROOM

Geez. What were the "recent events?"

I quickly washed up and went back into the lounge, where Liz was pouring the tea.

Gesturing over my shoulder with my thumb, I asked, "Hey, what happened in the bathroom? With a Ouija board?"

Renee snickered — I was sure happy to see that — and Liz let out a long sigh. "Oh. During our last Ouija workshop, a couple of customers decided they wanted privacy and took a board into the bathroom."

I nodded, taking a bite of my donut. "That makes sense. You don't want the boards to get ruined by water and bodily fluids. I understand."

"Well, that too," Liz continued. "But these customers accidentally conjured the spirit of a long-dead Cypress Grove city code inspector while in there unsupervised. And let me tell you, he takes his job very seriously, even in the afterlife."

"A ghostly bureaucrat," I mused. "Wow. What every new age shop needs."

Liz groaned. "He keeps materializing in the middle of my crystal healing sessions, muttering about 'improper plumbing fixtures' and 'unauthorized food and drink' because of our loose-leaf tea. Do you know how hard it is to align someone's chakras with a spectral clipboard-wielder hovering around?"

I couldn't help but snort-laugh. "Well, I suppose even the afterlife needs its red tape. Did he try to issue you a citation from beyond the grave?"

"Worse," Renee chimed in, reaching for a jelly-filled donut. "He started reorganizing Liz's entire inventory according to a filing system from 1978."

Liz rolled her eyes. "He couldn't believe I didn't have a Rolodex."

"Aww, poor dude," I said. "If only he knew about cell phones and the interwebs."

As we settled into our seats, sipping the delicious chamomile and lavender tea, my gaze was drawn to a small, leather-bound notebook sitting on the coffee table. It was nestled between a cluster of crystals and the donut box. My stomach clenched as I recognized it as Dominic's journal, the one Liz had snagged last night.

"So," I said, trying to sound casual, "how are you holding up, Renee? We were worried when you didn't respond to our texts yesterday."

Renee's face crumpled. "It's been awful. I'm definitely a prime suspect in Dominic's murder. The police kept me for hours, asking the same questions over and over. They seemed particularly interested in my magical abilities."

I nearly choked on my tea. "What? That's ridiculous! Is that even legal? You didn't do anything. And just because you have abilities doesn't mean anything."

Why were officers so interested in her? Then again, I recalled how Renee had left right at the break in pickleball play. She did have time to slip something into Dom's water, but why would she?

Liz nodded solemnly. "It gets worse. Marisol called me this morning. She strongly suggested Renee should lawyer up."

"Lawyer up?" I echoed, the gravity of the situation sinking in like a concrete block in quicksand. I sucked in a breath.

Renee's eyes welled with tears. "I didn't do anything wrong, I swear. Okay, maybe I used a teensy bit of magic during the pickleball game for that one serve, but I didn't kill Dominic. Why would I? I'd only met the guy that day."

I reached out and squeezed her hand. "We know that, sweetie. And we're going to help you prove it."

Renee both looked at me, her face filled with surprise and hope.

"Heck yeah we are," Liz asked.

"Of course we are," I said firmly. "That's what friends do, right? We stick together. Plus, I've got some experience with this detective stuff now."

Renee managed a watery smile. "Thank you. I guess Constance Winters is on my mind this month, and I really don't want to end up like her."

"You will *not* be wrongly accused of murder." I nodded toward the leather-bound notebook on the table and we all stared at it warily, like it was contaminated with E. coli. "Have you gone through Dominic's journal yet?"

The two women shook their heads.

Liz stirred a spoonful of honey into her tea. "We were waiting for you to get here before we dove in. It felt like something we should do together. It was hard to wait, though. That's why I texted and made it sound so urgent, so you'd get here right away."

She reached for the journal, her hands trembling slightly as she opened it. The spine crackled, and I caught a whiff of old leather and musty paper. The three of us huddled in closer on the sofa, our heads nearly bumping as we studied the pages.

"Geez Louise, his handwriting is worse than my doctor's," I muttered while staring at the scrawled notes.

Liz flipped through the first few pages. It appeared to be a diary, with handwritten dates at the top of every page.

"Looks like a lot of art stuff. Prices, gallery names, artist contacts. Nothing too juicy yet," Liz said, her tone disappointed.

We continued scanning, page after page filled with mundane details about paintings, sculptures, and gallery logistics. I was starting to worry that there was nothing useful when Renee gasped.

"Oh my goddess," she whispered, pointing to a page. "Look at this."

I leaned in closer, squinting to read the small handwriting. Liz did too.

"Do either of you need my readers?" Renee tried to untangle hers from atop her head.

"Yes," I said, and Renee handed me her glasses.

"No. I'm ok," Liz said. "Met S. for drinks. She's married, but who cares? It's a bit of fun. Note to self: her husband travels every other week. Perfect timing."

"Ewww," I said.

"Men are such pigs," Liz whispered, turning the page.

We found more entries like that, each one more cringe-worthy than the last. It was like reading the diary of a teenage boy, if that teenage boy was actually a middle-aged art dealer with the morals of a tomcat in heat. Renee and I passed the glasses back and forth so we could read.

"Gross," I muttered, feeling like I needed to bleach my eyes after looking at these pages. "No wonder he had 'women troubles,' as Jimbo put it."

As we delved deeper into the journal, the entries took an unexpected turn. Scattered among the art notes and conquest tallies were increasingly paranoid ramblings about witches and magic.

"I swear that new painting moved by itself," one entry read. "Is it cursed? Are the witches messing with me?"

Another passage caught my eye: "Saw a group of women in the park at midnight. They were dancing and chanting. I think they saw me. What if they cast a spell?"

"There are people doing spells all over town, at all hours," I said. "He was really losing it, wasn't he? Why was he so paranoid?"

Renee's face drained of its color. "This is bad. If the police see this, they'll think we, or me, had motive."

"I don't know about that," I frowned. The stress was obviously getting to our friend. "Seeing people chanting and dancing around town is pretty common. I don't that this ties us, or the coven, or any witches, really, to his death."

"And we didn't do anything," Liz protested. "*You* didn't do anything. He was paranoid. And ill-informed."

I chewed my lip, thinking. "On one hand, how would they prove magic? But from an outsider's perspective, I could see where it looks a little odd." I paused and added quickly, "but nothing that would hold up in a court of law."

We all looked from one to another and nodded. Then Liz's head whipped around and her voice turned sharp, like she was scolding a young child. She pointed. "No. Absolutely not. We are not doing this."

Renee and I turned in the direction of her outstretched index finger.

A shimmering figure was standing on the other side of the coffee table. I blinked, wondering if the Florida heat had finally fried my brain. But no, there it was in all its spectral glory.

The ghost of the city code inspector. My eyes widened.

He was decked out in a brown polyester suit that would have been appropriate in any 1970s office cubicle. His mustache was so thick and bristly, it looked like it could scrub barnacles off a boat hull. In one translucent hand, he clutched a clipboard; in the other, a ghostly pen poised to write.

"Ladies," he said, his voice echoing in a tinny way like he was speaking at a drive-thru fast-food place, "I must inform you that the consumption of food items in this area is a direct violation of code 7.3, subsection B of the Cypress Grove Municipal—"

Liz groaned. "Oh, for the love of — not now, Larry! We're busy."

The ghost huffed indignantly. "I'll have you know that proper food safety is a matter of utmost importance, ma'am. Is your husband or manager here to discuss the matter?"

"I'm in charge here. Your era was sometime during the Carter administration, and in the 21st century, women run and own businesses," Liz interrupted. She stood up, hands on her hips. "Larry, I appreciate your dedication, but we're in the middle of something important. You need to leave. Now."

Larry's spectral form flickered like a faltering lightbulb. "But... but the donuts! Think of the potential health code violations. It's thirty-five dollars a day per violation."

"The only violation here is you interrupting our meeting." Liz flicked her hands in his direction. "Shoo!"

Larry vanished, leaving behind only the faint scent of musty filing cabinets.

Liz flopped back onto the sofa, shaking her head. "I hate

being stern with spirits, but that guy is getting on my last nerve. He won't take a hint. I've tried doing various spells to help him move along but he's like Velcro."

"Like most men," I muttered, and we all burst into laughter, the tension from earlier momentarily forgotten. Then we refocused on the book and fell silent.

"Question," I said. "We know that Dominic was poisoned. Do we know with what?"

My friends shook their heads.

Liz reached for her phone. "I wonder... has anyone read the latest story in the paper? Zoe's article must be out by now."

She scrolled through her phone, then cleared her throat.

"Here's part of it," she said, and began reading aloud. " 'An autopsy report will be issued Monday, authorities say.' That's tomorrow. Let me think. How could I talk Chris into giving me that report?"

"Oh!" I perked up. "Oliver mentioned a while back that autopsy reports are public record in Florida. Anyone can request them."

Liz's eyes lit up. "Amelia, can you try to get that report tomorrow? I have an astrology class, and it's my first one since the surgery. I really shouldn't miss it. That way we don't have to involve Chris. Maybe you can stop by the medical examiner's office."

Renee turned to me with big puppy dog eyes. "Please? I have piano lessons I can't get out of. The recital is coming up soon."

I looked between my two friends, both giving me their best pleading expressions. How could I say no? Renee was too good of a person, and she was my coven leader. What good was a coven if we didn't all stick together?

Besides, the thought of digging deeper into this mystery was admittedly exciting. I wanted to know who poisoned Dom, killing him right in front of us.

"I'll take care of it. But we do have another problem."

"What's that?" Renee asked.

"We have stolen property here." I pointed at the book. "How are we handling that?"

"Oh!" Liz clapped her hands together. "I meant to tell you. You know that little bistro next door to Dominic's gallery?"

Renee and I nodded.

"Well, one of our coven members works there as a waitress. I was thinking that we could go there tonight and sneak in to put the book back."

I stared at Liz as if her third eye had suddenly opened and started winking at me. "Wait, what?"

Renee leaned forward, an intense look on her face. "But how are we going to get into the gallery without a key? Who works at the restaurant"

Liz's lips curved into a sly smile. "Amy."

"Oh. *Oh!*" Renee smiled and shook her head. "She's so talented."

When I looked back and forth between the two, Liz said quickly, "Amy's an expert in shadow melding."

She gave me a knowing look that made me feel like I was missing a crucial piece of information. What the heck was shadow melding?

I shifted uncomfortably in my seat. The idea of sneaking into the gallery was making me nervous, especially since we were in possession of stolen property — and you know, banned from the gallery by the police chief. This whole situation was starting to feel less like a fun mystery and more like a criminal conspiracy. One that could land us in prison for a long time — or at least a weekend in county jail.

"Hold on," Liz chimed in, holding up a hand. "Renee, you shouldn't go. You're already a suspect. If Amelia and I get caught, we might have a chance of getting out of trouble because of my relationship with Chris. You might not be so lucky."

I raised an eyebrow. "I'm not sure any of this is entirely legal, Liz."

Liz waved off my concern. "Details, details. So, you in? Tonight, after the bistro closes?"

I sighed, already feeling exhausted just thinking about it. "What time is that?"

"Ten," Liz replied, her eyes sparkling with excitement. "Amy said we could come a little early, though, and have a glass of wine."

I groaned internally. "You know I'm usually in bed by nine, right?" I paused, then reluctantly added, "But fine. I'll be there."

Nine

The last drops of Pinot Noir clung to my glass as I savored the fruity bouquet, trying to calm my nerves. Across the table, Liz nursed a glass of seltzer water. The Sage and Salt Bistro had long since closed, and a few busboys buzzed about, wiping down tables and stacking chairs. Amy had given us the wine and told us to hang tight while she did her closing routine.

The song "Kokomo" by the Beach Boys played a touch too loud over a hidden speaker.

I forced a weak smile. "I don't know about this, Liz. Breaking and entering?"

Liz touched the crystal pendant around her neck. "I know. It's not optimal. But—"

Before she could finish, a woman about our age approached our table. Amy, one of the coven members, looked like she'd been through the wringer. Her ash-blonde hair had frizzed and was slipping out of its ponytail, and dark circles lurked under her eyes. Despite the weariness etched on her face, she maintained an air of elegance.

Our coven was pretty large, and since I was a new member, I hadn't gotten to know everyone yet. Amy was among the people I'd barely chatted with.

"Greetings," she said, her voice barely above a whisper. "It's time."

My stomach clenched as we rose from our seats. This was my first foray into shadow magic, and honestly? I was terrified. I'd read a little about shadow magic online this afternoon and honestly, still didn't understand how it worked. We slipped out of the bistro and into a dimly lit hallway that connected to Dominic's gallery.

"I'm really not sure about this," I whispered, feeling my palms sweat. "What if we get caught? I've never broken into anywhere before."

As we stood in the hall, the other two women ignored my concerns.

Amy reached for our arms and squeezed. "I'll use shadow melding to get us inside. It's the art of becoming one with the darkness. Not invisibility, per se, but more like camouflage."

"What exactly does that mean?" Curiosity had momentarily overridden my anxiety.

Without answering, Amy let go of us and led the way. She paused at the corner, then stood with her back pressed against the wall. To my amazement, her form began to blur, melting into the shadows cast by the dim emergency lights.

She disappeared, right through the wall and into Dominic's gallery.

"No freaking way," I whispered, a mix of awe and apprehension washing over me.

Amy's musical, disembodied voice startled me. "The key is to clear your mind and feel the shadows around you. Let them envelop you, become a part of you. You're starlight, and walls mean nothing to starlight."

I wasn't really following her logic, but it sounded impressive. "Trippy."

"Shh!" Liz hissed. "Amy's in. Let's move."

The two of us crept along the hallway, our footsteps muffled by the carpet. I felt like I was in one of those Ocean's Eleven movies, minus the catsuit and night-vision goggles — or the confidence of a seasoned criminal.

While my stomach went into spin cycle mode, we reached a door in the hallway. It had a small sign on it that said "Dominic Harper Fine Art." There was a series of beeps, like an alarm was de-activating The lock on the door made a small *tha-thunk* sound. Did Amy's shadow magic include cracking alarm passwords? I was so confused.

I still couldn't get over how Amy had literally passed through a wall.

Then the door swung open, and we slipped inside, enveloped by the shadows Amy had conjured. The gallery was eerily quiet, the artworks on the wall looming in the semi-darkness. The place was lit only by the emergency exit sign, and it cast a spooky red glow.

Amy was fully visible now, and I reached to poke her arm. She was definitely in her corporeal form now.

"Sorry. Just checking," I said.

"I'll keep watch," she whispered. "You two return the book."

Liz nodded, and we tiptoed towards Dominic's office, my heart pounding so loud I was sure everyone in town could hear. I still couldn't get over Amy's magical abilities. We ducked under a ribbon of yellow crime scene tape across the doorway.

Once inside, Liz headed straight for the drawer where we'd found the book. We both used our sleeves to wipe down the leather journal thoroughly. I was glad I'd dressed for the occasion in all black: a long-sleeved cotton shirt and lightweight black pants.

I'd wanted to look the part, even if I felt like a fraud.

She pulled it open and began fiddling with the secret compartment, her brow furrowed in concentration.

"Rats," she muttered, struggling to get the book back into its hiding place.

I glanced nervously at the door, then back at Liz. A thought struck me. "Wait a second. Dom was probably the only one who knew about the secret compartment, right? Why not put it in the drawer?"

Liz paused, then chuckled softly. "Good point. Let's not reinvent the wheel while doing a B and E."

With a soft thud, Liz placed the book in the drawer and shut it, then wiped everything with her sleeve. I felt a wave of relief wash over me.

"Let's go," Liz said, already moving towards the door.

I shook my head, surprising myself. "Wait. While we're here, let's try to see what my psychometry tells us about any other objects."

Liz raised an eyebrow but nodded. "Now you're into this. How quickly you've turned to a life of crime."

While taking short, shallow breaths, I moved around the office, my fingers hovering over various items. Liz followed, carefully wiping everything that I touched with her sleeves and the hem of her shirt.

I was terrified of leaving fingerprints, but also desperate for any clue that might help us understand what was going on with Dominic. Most of the things I touched either inspired no visions, or mundane ones. I paused and concentrated hard for a few seconds on each object.

The pen showed Dominic writing. The letters revealed the mail lady. A coffee mug led to a vision of Dominic watching an art seminar on his laptop. None of it was useful or even interesting.

As I approached a low-slung black bookshelf, my hands tingled as I skimmed my fingertips across the wood. There, sitting innocuously among some knick-knacks, was a small, intricately carved wooden box.

"Hey, Liz," I whispered, "I think I've got something."

She hurried over, ready with her sleeve. "What is it?"

I reached out, my fingers skimming the smooth surface of the box.

Suddenly, I was no longer in Dominic's dimly lit office. Instead, I found myself in what looked like an expensive hotel room, bathed in soft light. My stomach dropped as I realized what I was seeing.

Dominic was there, but he wasn't alone. A woman I didn't recognize was close to him. They were gazing at each other with an intense intimacy that made me want to look away, but I couldn't.

She wore a nearly see-through pink negligee and downed an entire martini glass in one gulp.

He reached around her to the nightstand and grabbed a box, the one I was touching. "I brought you a little something, Sophia," he purred, handing it to her.

The woman opened it and laughed. "I can't. I'm sorry."

My breath caught as I saw what was inside: white powder.

She handed it back to him. Dominic dipped his pinky into the stuff and brought it to his nose, inhaling deeply. He closed his eyes, savoring the moment, then stuck his finger in his mouth and rubbed his gums.

"Oh, that's good stuff. Sure you don't want some?" he asked, dipping his finger in the powder and offering his pinky to her.

"No. But I want this." They kissed deeply, and I felt like a voyeur, unable to look away from this trainwreck. My face contorted into a grimace.

Dominic pulled back slightly, a manic glint in his eye. "What would Richard West do if he knew his wife was doing all this?"

She laughed, a low, throaty sound. "What he doesn't know won't hurt him," she said, pulling Dominic close again. She took his face between her hands. "I don't want you getting paranoid about what we're doing, though. You know how you get when you're on that stuff."

He replied with a murmur, and I thought he said something about "in control of things."

As they started to kiss more passionately, Dominic whispered something in her ear.

I couldn't make out the words, but judging by the woman's

yelp and laugh, I didn't want to know. They tumbled onto the bed, limbs entwined.

That was it. I couldn't take anymore. With a grunt, I dropped the box. It almost clattered to the floor, but Liz's quick reflexes caught it.

"Amelia?" Liz's concerned voice cut through my daze. "What happened? What did you see? Your face looks so strange."

I stared at her, my mind reeling from what I'd witnessed. How could I even begin to explain?

Before I could answer Liz, Amy materialized out of thin air, making me jump.

"Do you do that often? My goodness." I pressed my hand to my chest. "You scared me."

"We need to go. Now," she hissed, her eyes wide with urgency. "I heard you two being loud in here. Let's not take any stupid chances."

Liz and I exchanged panicked glances. We hustled out of the office and the gallery, Liz quickly wiping the doorknobs with her sleeve.

Back in the bistro, we paused to collect ourselves. I opened my mouth to spill everything I'd seen, but Amy held up a hand.

"I don't want to know," she said firmly. "For liability reasons. The less I know, the better."

Liz nodded. "Understood. Thank you, Amy. We owe you one."

I made a mental note to bring Amy a batch of cookies.

"Just be careful," Amy replied, her eyes darting between us. "Whatever you're mixed up in, watch yourselves. The coven can only do so much."

We said our goodbyes and stepped out onto the eerily quiet street. The air was still oppressively hot for this time of night, and it made my thoughts feel like they were swimming in soup. A faint headache throbbed at my temples, as it sometimes did when I had visions.

As we walked towards my car, I couldn't hold it in any longer.

"Liz, you won't believe what I saw. Dominic was with this woman, Sophia, and they were, ah, let's say it wasn't innocent. And get this. They mentioned a guy named Richard West. Apparently, Sophia is his wife. Oh, and there was cocaine. A small mountain of it."

Liz stopped and reached for my arm. "What? Richard West?"

"Yeah, why? Do you know him? Is he like a big drug dealer or well-known criminal or something?"

Liz's mouth hung open. "No, Richard West is a developer. He's one of the most influential people in town."

Ten

Breakfast the next morning was a big hit. Vegetable frittata with herbs, potato hash, and a special batch of mini muffins.

I was prepared for the guests to love the frittata, but everyone went wild over the muffins.

"So light, and not dry at all," one woman said, reaching for a second while her delicate Rolex glinted in the morning sunshine pouring through the window. "Is it one of your original recipes?"

"No. I'm more of a cookie expert, used to own a cookie delivery company in California. This is a simple, local recipe from the cemetery."

Her eyes lit up. "It's one of the gravestone recipes? I read about that in a tourist brochure yesterday."

I grinned and nodded, then went on to explain for the guests who looked confused. The Enchanted Eternity Park contained a wing where each gravestone was carved with a recipe. It had become something of a town competition to see who could put the most interesting dish on their headstone when they died. Folks closely guarded their final recipe, which was unveiled at their funeral service.

Some people went simple. Others erected large monuments and left behind detailed instructions. One lady who died last month had an entire Thanksgiving meal carved on the base of an obelisk.

"There's a group in town trying to publish a cookbook to raise money for more resources at the cemetery, because people around the world are starting to visit," I explained. "And I'll definitely lobby for this muffin recipe to be included."

Since the guests were so clearly fascinated by the recipes of the dead, I continued, telling them the origin story of the mini banana-prune muffins that were sitting in a cute basket lined with a gingham tea towel.

"This recipe came from a man named Basil Holloway. I'm told that for a while, he called these 'Banana-Plum Muffins,' because prunes have a negative connotation. But by the time he died, he felt that prunes had come into their own."

Everyone at the table was over the age of fifty, so they murmured and nodded appreciatively. This was a prune crowd. Heck, what was I talking about? I was in the prune demographic, too. I loved using dried fruits in recipes, and when I'd seen Basil's headstone, I knew I had to bake the delicate, spiced muffins for my guests.

After the guests left for their morning adventures, and following a quick cleanup, I found Jimbo, the inn's only employee. He was on the porch, lovingly spritzing a giant spider fern that he'd brought over a few weeks ago. It was hanging from the porch ceiling by a hook.

I wasn't sure why he was doing this, since the extreme amount of moisture in the atmosphere was surely enough to make the plant happy. The air practically dripped with humidity.

"I'll be gone for a little while, Jimbo."

"Sounds good, Miss Amelia."

"Liz and I have launched an investigation." I paused. "I'm going to the medical examiner's office for an autopsy report."

Jimbo, who was wearing jeans (even in this heat), and a green T-shirt with a gator on it that said "Don't Tallahassle Me," didn't miss a beat. "Okey-dokey. Do you need directions?"

I licked my lips, wondering why Jimbo knew the address of the M.E.'s office from memory. I decided to ignore that detail. "No, I've got my phone. I'll be back in a while."

It wasn't a far drive to the M.E.'s office, and I tried to feel confident as I walked in.

As I stepped through the automatic doors, a blast of frigid air hit me like a freight train made of ice. At first, I was grateful for the respite from the oppressive heat, but then I remembered why it was so cold in here. I shivered, and not only from the temperature.

The interior was as austere as a minimalist's dream gone wrong. Stark white walls, polished linoleum floors that squeaked under my sandals, and harsh fluorescent lighting that made everyone look like they belonged on an autopsy table themselves. The whole place had a sterile, chemical smell that tickled my nose and made my throat feel like it was closing.

I approached the front desk, where a receptionist was tapping away at a computer. Her name tag read "Brenda," and she had a perfectly coiffed blonde bob.

"Hi," I said, trying to sound more confident than I felt. "I'm here to request an autopsy report."

Brenda looked up, her expression unchanging. "Name?"

"Amelia Matthews."

She tapped the space bar on her computer keyboard. "No one here by the name Matthews. When did the person die?"

I blinked. "Oh. No, that's my name. I'm not dead."

"Clearly," she said.

"I'm looking for a report on Dominic Harper."

"Oh, yes, I've heard of that one." Her fingers flew over the keys. "Okay, here we go. Under Florida law, I'm able to give you the preliminary report for a fifteen-dollar fee."

I dug around my purse. Miraculously, I had the exact amount in cash, and I handed it to her.

She pointed to a row of hard plastic chairs that looked about as comfortable as a bed of nails. "Have a seat. Someone will be with you shortly with the report."

I sank down, immediately regretting my choice of a sundress. The cold plastic against my bare legs made me shiver again. I fiddled with my phone, pretending to be engrossed in something important while I waited. In reality, I was playing Candy Crush and trying not to make eye contact with the other person in the waiting area.

Why would anyone be sitting at the medical examiner's office on a Monday morning? Then again, why was I here? This caused my brain to spiral into a bit of an existential crisis.

After what seemed like an eternity, but was probably only five minutes, a door opened. A woman in a white lab coat emerged. My eyes widened as I recognized her. It was the medical examiner herself, Dr. Heather Yates.

I knew who she was, even though we'd never officially met. In fact, I'd been to her house. Well, her garage, to be exact. Oliver had introduced me to her son, Calvin. He was a local DJ who had helped me procure a radio that could broadcast to the dead.

Long story.

"Amelia Matthews?" she called out, glancing around the waiting area.

I stood up, smoothing my dress. "That's me."

Dr. Yates's eyes lit up. "Oh, you're Oliver's friend. I saw you at Pickled the other day. I wanted to say hello."

"You were a little occupied. With the deceased and all."

She smiled. "I've heard so much about you. I ran into Oliver at the food co-op the other day, and he was telling me all about you."

I smiled, feeling a mix of curiosity and mild awkwardness. "He's mentioned you as well. It's nice to finally meet you, Dr. Yates."

She laughed, a warm, happy sound that seemed out of place in the sterile environment. "All good things, I hope. And please, call me Heather. Let's go into my office to discuss the report you're requesting."

I followed her, not sure if I'd hit the jackpot, or if there were more surprises in store.

She led me down a short hallway and into her office. The moment I stepped inside, I felt like I'd been transported to a completely different world.

Unlike the cold, sterile waiting area, her office was warm and inviting. The walls were painted a soft yellow, and family photos adorned every available surface. A small sculpture of a frog in the corner bubbled water, and the shelves behind her desk were lined with heavy, leather bound books and framed photos. She also had a Nerf basketball hoop on the back of the door.

I recognized her older son, Calvin, in several of the photos. He was a lanky kid in his early twenties, about my daughter's age. Next to those were pictures of a younger child, presumably her other kid, grinning widely in various sports settings.

Dr. Yates's salt-and-pepper hair was cut in a stylish pixie that framed her face, making her look both mischievous and younger than her years. Despite the seriousness of her profession, lines crinkled the corners of her eyes. She looked like a woman who laughed a lot.

As she shrugged off her white lab coat and hung it on a nearby hook, I couldn't help but stifle a giggle. Underneath, she wore a vintage concert t-shirt from a 1980s hair metal band, complete with ripped sleeves and faded graphics. The shirt was such a contrast to the professional demeanor she'd showed in the waiting room.

Then again, that made sense to me. If you dealt with dead bodies daily, you'd have to bring some levity to the situation.

Catching my amused glance, Dr. Yates grinned. "What can I say? I'm a sucker for nostalgia. And Motley Crüe."

"The greatest decade for music, and you can't convince me otherwise."

She sat in a chair behind her desk, and she told a brief story about seeing Def Leppard's reunion tour. By now I felt like we were old friends.

"You know, I've met your son," I said. "He helped me with a..."

I tugged at my ear, trying to remember if Calvin — who went by the stage name of DJ Ghostwave — had mentioned if he told his mother about his spirit world broadcasting.

Heather twirled a pen in her fingers and laughed. "... a vintage radio? He's always helping people connect to ghosts."

"So, you know."

She nodded. "When we first moved here, I didn't exactly approve. I'm fine with it now. Sometimes with kids..." Her words faded into a sigh.

"I get it. My daughter's in college. She's twenty-one. Sometimes you have to let them live their own lives. Make their own mistakes."

"Communicate with their own ghosts."

We laughed. I truly liked this woman.

She cleared her throat. "Now, let's talk about why you're here. The Harper case. Very interesting, that one. Let me find the file."

She rifled through a stack of folders and slid one from the pile. "Here we go. Dominic Harper, white male, age fifty-five. Mild hypertension, but that's normal for a man his age. During the autopsy, we did find an unusual level of potassium in Mr. Harper's system. His myocardial cells showed signs of hyperkalemia, which isn't typically seen in cases of natural cardiac arrest."

I leaned forward. "Is that significant?"

She shook her head. "Not particularly. It's an interesting finding, but it doesn't tell us much about the cause of death on its own."

Irrationally, I hoped the poison was a rumor. Or a mistake. Then this entire situation would be put to rest and we could all move on with our lives. "What did kill him?"

Dr. Yates met my eyes. "Poison. Specifically, a toxin derived from a rare variety of oleander found only in Central Florida. It's not your garden-variety oleander. This is a subspecies that's particularly potent."

My mind reeled. Oleander? I'd seen those flowers all over town, their pink and white blossoms adding a cheerful touch to the medians and landscaping around town. But a rare, extra-poisonous variety? That seemed like something out of an Agatha Christie novel.

Or a town with a lot of magic.

"How rare are we talking?"

Dr. Yates leaned back in her chair. "Rare enough that whoever used it either has specialized botanical knowledge or connections to someone who does. This isn't something you'd stumble upon accidentally. I've seen regular oleander bushes around town, especially in Bicentennial Park, but I don't think any of them were this variety. I'm not a plant expert, though. I even killed a cactus once."

"Hunh." I was stumped. "Have you ever seen that as a cause of death before?"

She scrunched up her face and tapped her pen on the desk. "I don't think so. When I was an assistant M.E. down in Miami, I had a lot of mushroom poisoning cases. Never oleander, though."

The phone on her desk buzzed and the speakerphone crackled to life. "Dr. Yates, call on line four. It's the police chief."

"I'll be right with him," she said.

Yikes. That made me feel guilty somehow, even though I was doing nothing illegal at the moment. I definitely didn't want Chief Wolf to know I was here poking around. It was perfectly legal as a citizen to obtain a copy of an autopsy report — Florida had a solid open records law — but I didn't feel like explaining myself to anyone.

"Well, thanks." I stood up. "I appreciate it. I won't take up any more of your time."

"Wait, here's the report. I made a copy for you." She handed me three stapled-together pages. "Why don't we grab coffee or a drink sometime?"

"Absolutely, I'd love to," I said, adding that she could always find me at the inn. "It was good meeting you."

When I reached the door, I turned. "You know, I'm part of a Gen X group here in town. For women."

Dr. Yates looked up from her computer. "Oh, like the Junior League, or a women's club?"

"Sort of," I hedged. "It's more, ah, witchy."

"Oh. Sure. Because it's Cypress Grove."

"Yes. Exactly. It's more like a coven. We're always looking for new members. You don't have to be a full-fledged witch to join. It's a great group of women, and we have a lot of fun. Would you be interested in something like that?"

Heather's eyes lit up with curiosity. "A Gen X coven? That sounds intriguing. I've always been fascinated by the metaphysical, even if it doesn't always align with my scientific background. And I've had a difficult time meeting people since moving here, since my schedule is so wacky."

"We're a pretty diverse group," I explained. "We've got everyone from hardcore witches to skeptics who enjoy the company and the occasional tarot reading. No pressure to believe in anything you're not comfortable with."

She nodded, a smile playing at her lips. "You know what? That actually sounds like a lot of fun. I could use some female friendship that doesn't revolve around work or my kids."

"Great!" I beamed. "We have a meeting next week. The last meeting of the month is when prospective members can join in and ask questions. I'll text you the details if you give me your number."

"Sounds perfect." She jotted her number on a sticky note and rose to give it to me. "And who knows? Maybe my medical knowledge will come in handy for some of your investigations."

We shared a knowing look, and as I walked out, I did a mental fist pump. I felt like I'd made a valuable ally, and possibly a new friend.

Eleven

Exactly two hours later, I sat in a wicker chair on the porch of The Crescent Moon Inn. Liz and Renee were sprawled on the matching loveseat. Between us sat a worn wicker coffee table and a hastily assembled spread of cheese, crackers, grapes, and apples, along with some sweet cocktail pickles that Jimbo had canned himself.

We were shielded from the blazing afternoon sun, and a gentle breeze rustled the leaves of the oak tree that sat in the yard. It was almost pleasant, if you ignored the humidity that made my sundress cling to me like a second skin.

We were only out here because Renee had brought her dog. Bosco was a teenage chocolate lab, a gorgeous, vivacious creature with giant soulful eyes. Despite his happy personality, neither Renee nor I thought it best that he mingled with Freddie indoors. My cat wasn't used to dogs, Bosco wanted to chase every small animal in sight, and frankly none of us needed more stress today.

"Such a good boy," I said to Bosco and Renee. "Can I give him some cheese?"

"Sure. One cube's ok."

I reached for a piece of mild cheddar and Bosco sat patiently as I fed it to him. "So polite."

"Polite around everything that isn't smaller than him," Renee said.

We each nursed tall glasses of sweet tea, though mine was more ice than tea at this point. I'd been nervously crunching on the cubes while we pored over Zoe's latest article about the murder.

"Well, this is something," Liz muttered, tapping a blue-black manicured nail on the newspaper. (Liz' personal style was best described as "hippie witch.")

"Listen to this: 'Sources close to the investigation reveal that traces of an unidentified toxin were found in Dominic Harper's water bottle, recovered from the scene at Pickled.' "

She handed me the article. I brought it to my face, squinting at the small print. "Unidentified toxin? We know exactly what it is, thanks to Dr. Yates."

Renee, who had been mostly quiet, shifted uncomfortably. Her face was pale, and she kept fidgeting with the hem of her floral dress. I gave her a reassuring smile before setting the article down and reaching for another folder.

"This is the autopsy report," I said, flipping open the folder, "Dr. Yates confirmed that Dominic was poisoned with a rare variety of Oleander found only in Central Florida."

Liz's eyebrows shot up. "Oleander? Aren't those the pretty pink flowers all over town?"

I nodded. "Yep, but apparently this is some sort of super-poisonous subspecies. Not your average oleander you pick up at Home Depot. I doubt if anyone has it in their gardens."

"Don't be so sure," Renee said. "There are a lot of garden witches around town. People have some pretty incredible stuff growing around here, and I'm not just talking about marijuana."

"Great," Liz sighed, taking a long sip of her tea. "So, we're not only looking for a murderer, but a murderer with a green thumb and access to deadly flora. Those last two details narrow it down to a solid thirty percent of the town?"

She read through the report while muttering under her breath about rare art and rare plants.

Renee groaned and tipped her head back, causing Bosco to shift from me and the cheese to place his head on her knee.

"I can't believe this is happening. How did I get mixed up in all of this? All I wanted was to go out on a date with a guy who had a job and all his teeth. I feel defeated. You know, I work hard, try to do everything right, and what do I get? A murder investigation. If I hadn't used the bathroom when I did, I'd have a better alibi."

Liz and I exchanged worried glances. The weight of being a suspect — and her hectic, overworked lifestyle — had to be overwhelming.

"Hey," I said softly, trying to reassure her. "We're going to figure this out, okay? That's why we're here, going over all this information. We've got your back. Look, we're even organized for this case. I have a folder and a notebook."

After I said those words aloud, I realized how pathetically inadequate they were. Renee needed more than me and my notebook.

Liz nodded emphatically and squeezed Renee's knee that wasn't occupied by Bosco. "No one messes with our coven co-leader and gets away with it. Remember, you've got Amelia, who's solved three murders so far. She has a better track record than the cops. Well, almost. And I'm thinking we should do a murder board."

I shot Liz a look that said, 'not helping,' but Renee managed a weak smile.

"Thanks," she murmured. "I can't shake this feeling of dread. What if the police think I did it? I mean, they already do. I called three lawyers today and left messages. Not like I can afford any. What if-"

"Nope, we're not going down that rabbit hole," I interrupted, my voice firm but kind. "Let's focus on what we know and what

we can do. Like figuring out who might have access to this particular strain of oleander."

Renee cleared her throat. Liz and I paused to allow her to talk.
"Guys, I think I'm going to go home. This is too much for me. I
feel really exhausted all of a sudden. Maybe it's best if I'm not part
of the sleuthing. I don't know anything anymore."

"Oh, honey," Liz said, shifting so she could give Renee a
half hug.

I moved to the loveseat and wedged in on Renee's other side
so I could embrace her as well. "It's totally understandable that
you feel this way. Maybe a nice nap is in order. We can handle the
sleuthing."

After a few seconds, we all broke apart. Liz reached for
Renee's hands. She shut her eyes and launched into a spell in a
low, calm voice.

Goddess of comfort, hear our plea,
Ease Renee's worry, set her mind free.
Grant her peace and restful sleep,
Her spirit calm and heart deep.

A hot breeze kicked up through the leaves of the oak tree, as if
on cue. Renee's shoulders visibly relaxed, and some color had
returned to her cheeks.

"Thanks, you two." Renee smiled, and I already could see a
tiny sparkle had returned to her eyes. "I think I really do need that
nap."

Liz and I enveloped Renee in another group hug, careful not
to squish Bosco, who was trying to get in on the embrace. We
walked them to her minivan, which was parked in the inn's gravel
driveway. Bosco happily bounded into the back seat, his tail
wagging.

As Renee drove away, Liz and I stood on the porch, watching
until the minivan disappeared around the corner. The silence
hung heavy between us, broken only by the distant cawing of
crows.

I sighed, turning to Liz. "I feel terrible for her. This whole situation is such a mess."

Liz nodded, her eyes still fixed on the spot where Renee's van had vanished. "I can't figure out this oleander angle."

We trudged back to our seats on the porch, the cheerful spread of snacks now seeming out of place given our somber mood.

"We have to help her," I said firmly, reaching for my iced tea. "Whatever it takes."

Liz raised an eyebrow. "Whatever it takes? Even if it means more breaking and entering?"

I grimaced, remembering our foray into felonies at the gallery. "Okay, maybe not whatever it takes. How about whatever it takes within the bounds of the law? Or at least, you know, without risking arrest from your boyfriend?"

Liz guffawed. "Fair enough. We'll have to be clever about this. No more midnight raids or stealing evidence."

"Agreed," I said, nodding. "From now on, we play it smart. We gather information, we connect the dots, and we find out who really killed Dominic Harper. All without getting arrested or causing Renee any more stress."

As I stacked a cracker with two slices of cheese, Liz's phone pinged.

"Oh, crapola. That's Anne from Vintage Visions on Main Street. My dress is ready."

"Huh?" I held the cheese-cracker combo in the air.

She blew out a breath. "I promised Chris I'd attend this summer solstice charity event tonight. It's for a coyote sanctuary in town. Check out my dress."

Liz angled the phone so I could see the screen. It was a photo of a beautiful, pale blue tulle toga-like dress with rose gold accents.

"Gorgeous."

"I need to pick it up. And I have to swing by the florist for my flower crown."

"That sounds fun. Maybe you'll come across some gossip about Dominic."

"Yeah, that's what I was thinking."

"In the meantime, I'll make a list of suspects and details and email you. How about that?"

"Perfect. Actually, text me. I'll be running around and I can read texts easier. Haven't figured out how to make the font bigger on my phone email."

Once Liz left and I cleaned up the remnants of our snacks, I went inside. While still mulling over the possible suspects in Dominic's death, I puttered about the inn, taking care of a few little details before I sat down to type out all my theories. Sometimes cleaning really helped get my thoughts straight.

I was halfway through dusting the lobby when Jimbo walked in. He was with his girlfriend, Sage, who was Oliver's younger sister. They'd been dating a few months. At first, I thought it was an odd pairing — Sage considered herself a cowboy witch, and Jimbo was a classic Florida Man. He'd never met a gator or a free beer T-shirt that he didn't love.

He was also a plant shaman, a fact I remembered when he called out a booming "howdy."

I gave Sage a quick hug, making sure to avoid being poked with the brim of her straw cowboy hat.

"Just the man I want to see. I have a plant question for you."

He grinned. "Well, shoot, Miss Amelia. What's on your mind? Did Freddie get into the special catnip stash again?"

I chuckled, remembering the time Jimbo had brought over some extra-potent nip. "No, nothing like that. I'm curious about oleander. Specifically, a rare, extra-poisonous variety that's supposed to be native to Central Florida."

Jimbo's eyes widened, and he let out a low whistle. "Woo-wee, that's some heavy stuff you're askin' about."

Sage raised an eyebrow. "Sounds pretty serious. I'd like to listen in but I'm only here to drop him off. I have a job interview today."

Now that I studied her, I did notice that Sage was in a rather conservative navy-blue dress. She also wasn't wearing her signature cowboy boots. Instead, she wore a demure pair of tan heels.

"Good luck with the interview. What's the job?"

"It's for a secretary at a law firm. That's what I used to do, a long time ago."

"Well, you look gorgeous. Good luck." I paused. "Um, you might not want to wear the hat."

Sage winced. "Doesn't go with the business dress?

I shook my head.

"Okie dokie." She took off her hat and handed it to Jimbo. "Keep it safe for me, willya?"

She and Jimbo rubbed noses and walked out. They were weird, but cute.

Jimbo turned to me, his usually jovial expression now serious. He lowered his voice, as if sharing a secret. "Oleander? Are you sure?"

I nodded and went to the desk where I'd set down the folder with the autopsy report. "Check this out. Dominic Harper died from oleander poisoning."

I handed him the file and he went through it, his eyes widening. "This particular oleander ain't common at all, Miss Amelia. It's a nasty piece of work, even by oleander standards. Most folks 'round here won't touch it with a ten-foot pole."

"Really? Why's that?"

"Well," Jimbo said, scratching his stubbly chin, "there's a lot of lore surrounding that plant. Florida witches and other magical types have steered clear of it for generations. It's too dang deadly, even for them. Legend has it that back in the thirties, a powerful witch tried to use it in a spell over in Tampa and ended up wiping out half her coven by accident."

Goosebumps formed on my arm. "That's terrifying. But if it's so rare, and if so many people avoid it, how would someone even get their hands on it?"

Jimbo glanced around, as if checking for eavesdroppers, then leaned in closer. "Now, I ain't one for gossip, but there's been talk for years about a greenhouse outside town limits, out in the county. Rumor has it they grow all sorts of rare and dangerous plants there, including that particular oleander. I've never been there, because frankly, I'm not interested in dark magic like that. I steer well clear of that kind of stuff. As should you."

Maybe because of Jimbo's warning, or in spite of it, I viewed this as an opportunity. This could be the lead we needed. "Do you know where exactly this greenhouse is?"

Jimbo shook his head. "Nah, can't say I do. It's one of those things everyone's heard of, but nobody seems to know exactly where it is or who runs it. Kinda like the Bermuda Triangle of Cypress Grove, if you catch my drift."

"Thanks, Jimbo. This is really helpful."

He grinned, seemingly pleased to have been of assistance. "Happy to help, Miss Amelia. But, uh, maybe don't go poking around too much, you hear? That plant ain't nothing to mess with. Even us plant shamans give it a wide berth."

"Understood. I'll be careful."

But as I said those words, I was already trying to figure out how to find a place that apparently didn't want to be found.

Twelve

The rest of the afternoon flew by. I scrubbed bathrooms until they sparkled, changed linens with military precision, and tackled a mountain of bookkeeping that had been looming for days. Innkeeping was way harder than I anticipated, but it was also satisfying. By the end of the day, I had tangible results of everything I'd accomplished — and so far, happy guests.

Between tasks, I fired off a series of texts and emails to various coven members and witches around town, trying to be as subtle as a sweaty perimenopausal woman could be when inquiring about deadly plants.

To Marisol:

> "Hey, lady! Quick question. Any interesting herbs or flowers you've come across lately that aren't exactly garden variety? Asking for a friend. Ok, I'm asking for me. I'm searching for a greenhouse, maybe one that's bigger and outside of town. Heard of anything like that?"

To Midge, a cranky older woman who ran an antique store:

"Good afternoon! Hope your joints aren't giving you too much trouble in this humidity. Random thought: ever heard of any unusual greenhouses in the area? Maybe something off the beaten path?"

To Luna, one of the coven's green witches who also loved to talk and gossip:

"Luuuuna! Miss your face! Quick botanical question. What's the most exotic plant you've ever worked with? Any fun stories? I'm looking to get into some gardening. Any suggestions for greenhouses?"

I tried to keep things light and casual, peppering my messages with emojis and inside jokes. No need to let on that I was investigating a murder. Just your average middle-aged innkeeper with a sudden, intense interest in rare flora.

As I finished cleaning the last guest room, my phone buzzed, and I slipped it from my apron pocket. I liked to wear a durable canvas apron with lots of pockets when I cleaned.

It was a text from Luna. I chewed on my bottom lip as I opened the message, hoping for a lead.

Ciao Amelia! Exotic plants, huh? Well, the most interesting ones I've worked with came from a farm stand-slash-nursery. It's this huge greenhouse complex out on County Road 17, past the old Johnson farm. But be careful if you go there. The owner, Donna Anderson, is known for her unconventional methods. Some say she dabbles in the darker sides of plant magic. Unlike most of the witches in the area, she's not a member of any coven. I'd stick to the farmer's market for your gardening needs, hon. Safer that way. But if you do go, she has a killer farm stand. Best eggs in the county. Packed with Omega 3s.

I stared at the message, a mix of excitement and apprehension swirling in my stomach. This sounded exactly like the kind of place that might cultivate rare oleander — and a lot like the place Jimbo had described. And this Donna Anderson character? Was she a suspect, or merely a deadly plant dealer?

But Luna's warning gave me pause. What did she mean by "unconventional methods" and "darker sides of plant magic"? I'd seen some pretty wild things since moving to Cypress Grove, but the idea of tangling with a dangerous plant witch made me nervous.

Still, if this greenhouse held the key to solving Dominic's murder and clearing Renee's name, I had to check it out. I'd have to be careful. Maybe bring backup. And definitely wear closed-toe shoes.

As I saved the information in my notes app, another text came through, this time from Midge:

"Amelia, dear, my joints are fine, thank you for asking. As for greenhouses, stay away from that place on CR 17. The egg prices are outrageous. Now, about those lace curtains you promised to look at for me..."

I chuckled, imagining Midge's gruff voice. Two warnings about the same place in as many minutes? Now I *definitely* had to investigate.

Setting my phone down, I glanced at the clock. It was nearly time for cocktail hour, and I had a lot to do. I expected the four guests that were staying with me would be back soon for wine and snacks, so I moved to the kitchen to prepare.

I bustled around, arranging an assortment of cheeses, crackers, and fresh fruit on a platter. As I uncorked a bottle of local white wine, I heard the front door open, followed by the cheerful chatter of my guests returning from their day's adventures.

For the next hour, I played the gracious host, refilling glasses and listening to tales of psychic readings and ghost tours. This was the part of the day I loved the most — hanging out with guests, laughing, living in the moment. By the time they retreated to their rooms to freshen up for dinner, I was almost hungry myself, and pondered whether to order pizza.

Instead, I tackled the mess in the kitchen, loading the dishwasher and wiping down counters. Before I knew it, the grandfather clock in the library chimed seven times. I blinked in surprise, realizing I'd lost track of time.

Just then, my phone chimed with a text. It was from Liz, and the message made me do a double-take.

YOU NEED TO GET HERE NOW

I frowned and texted back. I'd never received this many messages from Liz in all caps in one week.

Where? And why?

Liz called seconds later and didn't even start with a hello. "The charity event. For the coyote sanctuary. You need to come here. Now."

"Why are you whispering?"

"Because I ducked behind a topiary and I don't want anyone to hear me."

"Oh." I paused, trying to be logical. "Why do I need to come there?"

"Because Sophia and Richard West are here. You can gather clues. And I've got news."

I licked my lips, feeling like I was missing a key piece of context. "Can't you gather the clues since you're already there? And what's the news?"

"No," she hissed. "I'm with Chris. Oh crap, there he is. I gotta go. Get your butt over here. And oh: wear something solstice-like."

"W-wait. What about a ticket?"

There was a millisecond of silence. "We'll leave your name at the door. Chris is a big donor to the coyote sanctuary, so if we say someone should enter, they'll let you in."

She hung up, leaving me staring at my phone.

Something solstice-like? What did that mean?

Thirteen

I burst into the charity ball like a cross between a discount store Aphrodite and a flower shop explosion.

My flowing white bedsheet-turned-dress, hastily draped over a long, ivory peignoir that I'd found in a closet, was secured with a gaudy plastic brooch. The ensemble billowed around me as I entered. The look might have been passably ethereal if not for the makeshift crown perched precariously on my head, a hodgepodge of slightly wilted daisies, pink roses, and baby's breath I'd pilfered from the days-old bouquet at the inn's front desk. I'd woven them together with floral wire in what I hoped was an artful arrangement.

It all looked snazzy in the mirror back in my bedroom, but based on the confused glances I was getting, I had a sneaking suspicion I was way off.

To complete my solstice-goddess ensemble, I'd slipped on my only pair of gold, strappy sandals. They were gladiator-style and a bargain bin find from several years ago. A strand of fake pearls and some hastily applied glittery green eyeshadow completed the look.

The moment I stepped into Studio 407 — the town's most upscale event venue — I realized how out of place I was. I'd been to this building before, for a charity movie night. Oliver and I had watched Casablanca while drinking wine, as a fundraiser for local youth theater.

But tonight, the place had been transformed into a magical solstice garden. Lush greenery and vibrant wildflowers cascaded from the exposed rafters of the 16-foot ceilings. In the center of the room stood a massive stone fountain, water trickling over its tiers. Floating candles bobbed in the basin, casting shadows across the Brazilian hardwood floors.

To my left, a long table groaned under the weight of an elaborate spread provided by one of the venue's caterers. Platters of fresh fruits and vegetables were artfully arranged around a towering cake decorated to look like a lifelike and detailed coyote. A chocolate fountain burbled, surrounded by mountains of dippable treats.

My gaze lingered on the mounds of marshmallows, apple slices, and brownie bites. I adored a well-stocked dessert fountain.

And the guests had clearly gone all out. Women in flowing gowns of gossamer and silk twirled across the dance floor, their hair adorned with intricate floral crowns. Men sported linen suits or realistic-looking togas, and nearly all the guys had laurel wreaths on their heads. Laurel. That's what I'd missed in creating my crown. Crud.

Through the arched doorways, I could see the outdoor brick and bamboo courtyard, where even more guests mingled under romantic fairy lights and towering 30-foot bamboo plants. The scent of something tasty wafted through the air. Man, the catering for this event must have cost tens of thousands. Was that lobster? I squinted at a buffet table.

I tugged at my makeshift toga-dress, feeling like I was dressed for a college frat party rather than a high-class charity event. As I scanned the crowd for Liz, my eyes were drawn to the upstairs balcony, where more elegantly dressed guests sipped cocktails. The men up there were in tuxedos, and the women in actual ball gowns.

This was all so weird. And for coyotes, no less. Giant, black-

and-white posters of mangy-looking animals lined one wall. Poor things.

I pulled my phone out of an old, white evening handbag. I'd unearthed the purse in one of the suitcases I'd brought from California but had yet to sort and put away because it was filled with formalwear. While trying to blend into a potted plant, I quickly texted Liz.

I'm here, where are you? I'm standing to the left of the chocolate fountain.

Be right there, don't move.

While I waited, I took a few steps toward the fountain, grabbing a stick and spearing a strawberry. I plunged it into the flowing milk chocolate. After I'd coated it thoroughly, I took a bite. *Yum.* The coyote charity did not skimp on the chocolate quality. I finished the fruit and went for another. I was savoring a chocolate marshmallow when I spotted Liz power-walking over.

"We don't have a lot of time," she said quickly.

"Hunh?" I said through a mouthful of marshmallow.

She paused for a beat and eyed my crown. "Dystopian. I love it. Impressive how you threw all that together in less than an hour. It's like Summer Solstice meets The Purge."

I wasn't entirely sure what she meant since I'd never seen The Purge — I hated scary movies, she loved them — so I wasn't entirely sure what she was talking about. "Thanks. So where are Richard and Sophia West? Have you talked with them?"

"I have." Liz's eyes didn't just dance with delight. They positively disco-ed. "Chris and I were introduced to them by the town council president. We had a nice chat. Here's the thing: Sophia seems, I dunno... weird."

"Weird how?"

She shook her head. "Let me tell you the news first. Chris stepped down from the Harper homicide."

I gaped. "Wait. What? Why?"

"A conflict of interest." She took a long sip from her glass of sparkling water. "He said it wasn't right to investigate since I'm technically involved. He called in the Florida Department of Law Enforcement."

"I don't know what that is."

She waved her hand dismissively. "It's like the state police, but not. They provide investigative services to local departments and such. They also have a crime lab."

"I see." Yikes. I hoped we'd wiped all of our prints off the surfaces in Dominic's office. Explaining away our presence to local cops was one thing, but to a more experienced, serious agency? I shivered.

"Anyway, they've sent a detective to town. Chris doesn't know her. She's looking into Dominic's past, apparently. And Renee's."

"Did Chris tell you that?"

Liz shook her head. "I heard it from a friend who knows a dispatcher."

That seemed tenuous. "Okay. Let's get back to Sophia West. Why is she weird?"

"Well," Liz said, gesturing with her water glass, "she's been huddled in corners all night having intense conversations with Jack — you know, from the pickleball game? Every time Richard West comes near them, they spring apart like teenagers caught behind the bleachers. And get this: I overheard her telling someone she was in Miami last week, but Dominic's journal definitely mentioned meeting her for drinks three days ago."

Did that mean anything? Given Dom's cocaine habit, who knew if we could trust the journal or his version of events? Or this Sophia person.

"Odd. What does she look like?" I squinted at the crowd. "I want to make sure I spot the right woman."

"She's wearing this amazing emerald green dress — very Grace Kelly — and has her hair up in a complicated twist. She looks like she has a stylist on staff."

"We're practically twins in that department," I deadpanned.

Liz snickered. "Oh, and she's got this incredibly unique necklace. It looks antique, like something from an estate sale. Big emeralds to match her dress. When I complimented it, she got all flustered and changed the subject."

I was about to ask more about the necklace when Chief Wolf appeared beside us, looking dashing in a crisp, flax-colored linen suit and laurel wreath. His usually stern expression was gone as he slipped an arm around Liz's waist.

"Ladies," he said, nodding at me. "Interesting costume, Amelia."

I tugged self-consciously at my bedsheet. "Thanks. I'm really into DIY."

"The coyotes don't judge," he said with a wink. "Speaking of which, did you see the mother and pups we rescued last week? They're in the video playing on the back wall."

Liz brightened. "Oh, they're adorable! The way the littlest one keeps trying to howl but squeaks instead."

"Those pups would've died if the sanctuary hadn't found them," Wolf added. "Their den was flooded out during that big storm."

I nodded politely, but my attention had drifted to scanning the crowd. Through the sea of flowing dresses and formal wear, I spotted Jack and Sophia near the courtyard doors, their heads close together in what appeared to be another secretive conversation.

"If you'll excuse me," I said, already backing away, "I think I see someone I need to talk to."

Fourteen

As I inched through the crowd in the room, I silently thanked my past self for choosing comfortable sandals.

I wove through the crowd toward the hors d'oeuvres table, trying to look casual. The table was set with fancy finger foods arranged in geometric patterns that seemed too artistic to disturb. Still, I needed a reason to hover near Jack and Sophia's not-so-secret meeting spot.

They looked like old pals. Did they know each other through Dominic?

Grabbing a small plate, I started loading up on vegetables. One carrot stick for camouflage. Two for authenticity. Five more because, well, I was actually getting hungry. Some celery. More carrots. *Ooh, ranch dip!*

By the time I'd positioned myself beside a massive fern out of eyesight — but not earshot — of the conspirators, my plate looked like I was catering a rabbit's birthday party.

Just as I caught a snippet of Jack saying something about "the necklace," a voice beside me almost made me drop my vegetable tower.

"Planning to feed a family of herbivores? Not that it's a bad thing. I'm vegan, myself."

I turned to find myself face-to-face with a guy who looked like he'd stepped out of a Mediterranean travel magazine. Dark curly hair, olive skin, and the kind of smile that probably got him out of speeding tickets.

"Oh, I, uh…" I shifted my weight, trying to maintain my strategic eavesdropping position while not looking like I was having a love affair with baby carrots. "I'm very passionate about vitamin A."

He laughed. "That's good. You'll have excellent night vision. Helpful for keeping an eye on things." He winked, and I couldn't tell if he was flirting or if he'd somehow caught onto my amateur sleuthing.

I forced a laugh, straining to hear Jack and Sophia's conversation while attempting to look engaged with Mr. Mediterranean. If I leaned slightly to my left, I could barely make out Sophia's voice, though Jack's reply was lost in the noise of the party.

"I'm Luca," the guy said, extending his hand. "And you must be Persephone, goddess of raw vegetables?"

Okay. If I played this right, I could maintain my position and keep an ear on the suspects. "Actually, I'm Amelia. And these aren't all for me. I'm sharing with this fern. He's on a diet."

I had absolutely zero interest in this man, but if I could get him to talk, I'd have a good excuse to linger. Fortunately, getting men to talk wasn't that difficult.

"So, you from around here?" I smiled sweetly.

Luca launched into a story about moving to Cypress Grove with his sister for a job at some tech startup, but I was only half-listening. Who knew there were tech start-ups in town?

He was dressed in what appeared to be a designer toga that probably cost more than my monthly car payment, with golden cords wrapped artfully around his biceps. A laurel crown sat perfectly on his dark curls, making my wilted flower arrangement feel even more pathetic.

"…and that's when I realized Florida isn't just theme parks and gator farms," he finished with a gleaming smile.

"Mm-hmm," I murmured, tilting my head to catch Sophia's words. "Cypress Grove is a great town, isn't it?"

"...can't keep avoiding this..." I heard her say to Jack. "...the necklace isn't..."

"So, what do you do?" Luca asked, moving closer. Close enough that I caught a whiff of expensive cologne.

"I run an inn," I said distractedly. Jack was saying something about "next week" and "once things are settled."

Luca's eyes lit up. "That's fascinating! I'd love to hear more about it over drinks sometime."

Record scratch. Wait. What? I stared at Luca with my mouth slightly open.

Oh.

Oh no.

The reality of the situation hit me like the heat that loomed outside the door. This gorgeous young man was actually flirting with me. Me, a woman old enough to have babysat him. He couldn't be more than twenty-five, tops. I had crow's feet older than him.

"I need to use the ladies' room," Sophia announced loudly enough for me to hear clearly, her voice a touch shaky. Finally!

"That's so sweet," I said to Luca, already backing away, my plate of carrots threatening to avalanche. "But I, uh, need to powder my fern. It was nice meeting you!"

I scurried away, leaving him looking confused, probably wondering if fern-powdering was some kind of older woman euphemism he'd never heard of. Behind me, I heard him call out, "But what about drinks?"

Sorry, kid. I had a suspect to tail and a murder to solve. And a boyfriend who I adored. Oliver's age and wisdom was so much more appealing than this young, puppy-dog guy.

I kept my eye on Sophia and her beautiful emerald dress as we made our way through the party and toward the restrooms. When I burst into the bathroom, I was still carrying the plate of food (although I think I'd lost a carrot stick somewhere on the edges of the dance floor).

There was rustling from the handicap stall. I quickly locked the main door — a move that probably violated several fire codes and criminal laws, but desperate times called for desperate measures. I set my rabbit buffet on the marble counter and surveyed myself in the mirror.

Naturally, there was a glob of ranch dressing on my toga, right at chest level. As I dabbed at it with a paper towel, I heard the toilet flush.

Sophia emerged from the stall in a sweep of emerald silk, the necklace glinting at her throat. Up close, she was even more elegant than Liz had described, like she'd stepped out of a vintage fashion magazine. Of course, I recognized her from the bawdy vision I'd had. Inwardly I cringed, thinking of her in lingerie and nibbling on Dom's ear. *Shudder.*

"Oh, I love your crown!" she gushed, moving to the sink beside me. "So creative. Much more interesting than these cookie-cutter laurel wreaths everyone else is wearing."

I touched my wilting daisies self-consciously. "Thanks. I like to think of it as artisan chic."

Sophia smiled, reaching into her clutch to pull out an ornate silver compact. As she checked her lipstick, I pretended to stumble slightly, bumping into her.

"Oh gosh, sorry!" I giggled, doing my best impression of someone who'd had too much wine. "Those chocolate-covered strawberries must've been stronger than I thought."

The compact clattered to the counter and I snatched it up. "Here, let me—"

The moment my fingers closed around the cool metal of the compact, the bathroom vanished. I was suddenly in Dominic's gallery after hours, the space lit only by security lights. Sophia stood before Dominic, tears streaming down her face.

"You promised you'd give it back," she pleaded while holding the compact, as if he'd interrupted her while she was reapplying lipstick. "The necklace belonged to my grandmother. I only let you authenticate it, not sell it!"

Dominic's laugh was cruel, and in that instant, I hated him for how he had treated Sophia. "Sweetheart, that necklace paid for a lot of bad habits. But here's the thing. It wasn't your grandmother's. It was a fake, like most of the pieces in this gallery."

"You're lying." Sophia's voice turned hard. "I know you sold the real one. And I know about the other forgeries. Thompson's been watching you."

Dominic's face contorted with rage. "Thompson? My landlord? That nosy bastard's been in my business?"

"He owns this whole building, Dom. Did you really think he wouldn't notice the late-night deliveries?"

"That explains why he's been raising the rent." Dominic grabbed her arm. "Is he blackmailing you too? Is that why you're here?"

The vision ended abruptly as Sophia yanked the compact from my grasp. But I'd seen enough. The necklace she was wearing now — was it the real one or a fake? And more importantly, who was this landlord? If he knew about Dominic's forgery operation and was pressuring him for money, perhaps he was a suspect.

I stared at Sophia. She stared right back, her big eyes unreadable. Then, to my complete surprise, she reached up and removed one of the wilting daisies from my crown.

"For luck," she said softly, tucking it into her complicated updo. "We all need a little of that these days, don't we?"

Liz was right. Sophia was weird. Ethereal, definitely. Maybe on something. Who knew.

She turned to leave, but the door had obviously been locked. By me. A flash of something —panic? annoyance? — crossed her face before she composed herself. "Ah, these old buildings. The doors stick sometimes."

I watched as she efficiently worked the lock, her movements precise and practiced. She slipped out without another word, leaving behind only the faint scent of expensive perfume and about a million questions.

I pulled out my phone and fired off a quick text to Liz:

> Pretty sure I just massively screwed up. Found our suspect but let it walk right out the door. Meet me by the chocolate fountain in 5?

While I waited for a response, I washed my hands, reapplied some lipstick, and sighed hard.

Liz texted a thumbs up, my cue to leave. When I emerged from the bathroom, a male voice made me jump.

"There you are!" Luca was leaning against the wall with a practiced, saucy smirk on his face. "I was worried you and your fern might need assistance with the powdering. And I got us a plate of fruit."

He held out a green plastic plate of melon balls.

Great. Exactly what I needed. A man in his twenties with expertly gelled hair who apparently didn't understand when a woman was letting him down easy. Though to be fair, "I need to powder my fern" probably wasn't the clearest rejection in dating history.

"Uh, Luca," I said. "I don't know if you've noticed, but I'm old enough to be your mother."

His smirk unfurled into an eager grin. "I like older women."

Oh dear. I wasn't in the mood for men's egos or libidos or fetishes this evening. "I'm taken."

The grin crumpled. "Oh. I'm sorry."

He looked genuinely embarrassed.

"Hey, no worries," I said kindly, feeling bad for the kid. His face had that crestfallen look that reminded me of my daughter's high school boyfriend when she'd dumped him before college. "You seem like a nice guy. Really."

Then it hit me like a wet towel to the face. Here I was, trying to solve a murder, and I had a chatty twenty-something who might know people in town. What was wrong with me?

"Actually," I said, "can I ask you something? Do you know Sophia West?"

His eyes lit up. "Oh yeah, she's friends with my sister, who teaches at that fancy new Pilates studio downtown. The one with the crystal-infused water. Sophia goes there every day. I mean, look at her body."

Bingo.

"Really?" I tried to keep my voice casual while plucking a melon ball off his plate. "What's she like? She seems..." I paused, pretending to search for the right word. "Interesting."

I popped the melon into my mouth.

"Totally interesting," Luca agreed. "She's always organizing these cool charity events like tonight. And she knows everyone. Like, everyone. Apparently she used to throw wild parties, but she stopped that recently. Lately she's been kind of stressed. My sister said she lost some family heirloom or something."

I nearly choked on my cantaloupe. "An heirloom? Like jewelry?"

"Yeah, maybe. Hey..." A sly grin spread across his face. "I might know more. But information comes with a price."

Oh boy. Here we go.

"Luca," I said firmly, "I can't date you. I have a boyfriend, and more importantly, I'm old enough to remember when MTV played music videos."

"They did?" A confused look crossed his unlined face.

"Yes. Tell me about Sophia."

"But maybe you know someone your age? Honestly, I'd like to go on a date. Like an old-fashioned date. Dinner and a movie. I hate using apps."

I thought quickly. This was for Renee, right? To clear her name? And technically, playing matchmaker wasn't illegal. Unlike, say, breaking into art galleries or stealing journals.

"Tell you what," I said, "I belong to a group of women — we're all Gen X. So, we're old. Old-er. I promise I'll try to set you up with someone available and fun, who appreciates a young guy who brings her fruit."

His face brightened. "Really? Deal! Okay, so here's what I know."

Luca leaned in closer, lowering his voice. "My sister told me that last week, Sophia had an intense phone call in the studio's changing room. She was talking about proving something belonged to her family. Kept saying she had documentation and 'provenance' or whatever that means. Got really worked up about it."

My pulse quickened. "What kind of documentation?"

"That's the weird part. My sister said Sophia kept mentioning her grandmother and some kind of paperwork from Europe. Then she started crying about how 'he' was going to expose everything if she didn't pay up. She's been totally off since that day. Missing classes, showing up looking stressed. And get this." He handed me the plate of melon. "Yesterday she completely lost it when another client complimented her necklace. Like, full-on panic attack in the middle of class."

The hair on the back of my neck stood up. Blackmail? And a necklace again.

"When did all this start?" I asked, trying to keep my voice steady.

"Let me think." He tapped his chin. "About three weeks ago? My sister said she came to Pilates looking like she'd seen a ghost. My sister loves to gossip." He shook his head. "She's incorrigible. Tells me details about people I don't know. It gets annoying."

I tuned Luca out for a few seconds. *Three weeks ago.* Was that around the time Dominic sold her grandmother's necklace, according to my vision?

"I'm fascinated that your sister knows this much about Sophia," I said.

Luca shrugged. "Yeah, well, rich people love to talk during Pilates. Especially when they're on those weird machines that look like torture devices."

I filed that information away, my mind already racing with possibilities. A greenhouse that grew deadly plants. A woman with a grudge. And a dead man.

"Great," I said briskly, handing the plate back to him. I paused to dig around in my handbag and pulled out a business card. "I run the Crescent Moon Inn. Call me if you or your sister have more info."

As he stammered something about putting my "digits" into his phone and texting me his "deets," I gave him a wave, a wink, and a smile, and went to brief Liz.

Fifteen

The Sunny Side Up Diner sat on County Road 17, a cheerful yellow building that looked like it had been transported straight from the 1950s. A neon sign in the window blinked "OPEN 24 HRS" in faded pink, though the N flickered. The parking lot was half-full of pickup trucks and sedans, a mix of locals getting their Tuesday morning coffee and tourists fueling up before hitting the theme parks.

Normally on weekdays I attended to the guests, cooking an elaborate breakfast and cleaning. Today, however, other duties called. Although I'd cooked a morning feast for my guests, Jimbo was serving it — and entertaining the guests with some plant shaman knowledge.

I pulled my car next to Liz's white Kia Soul, careful to avoid a pothole the size of one of my guest's Louis Vuitton suitcases. Speaking of guests, I had a honeymooning couple from Wisconsin who were hilarious to have around.

"The newlyweds are so sweet," I told Liz as we walked toward the diner's entrance. Maybe small talk would calm my nerves. "They got married at that wedding chapel in town. The bride still has blue glitter in her hair from her showgirl-themed bachelorette party."

"Good luck to her, she's going to need it. Marriage is rough," Liz said, pulling open the door. A bell jingled overhead.

"Does this mean I won't be a bridesmaid for you and Chris?" I joked.

We slid into the last open booth. Somehow, even though the place was packed, we were lucky enough to get a table. I'd been noticing lately that stuff like this happened frequently. Parking spaces on crowded streets, sold out items magically appearing, checkout lanes opening right when I needed. I wondered if this was luck, or something more mystical at work.

Either way, I felt like the universe had my back.

"Uh, no. Neither of us want to hurry our relationship," Liz said. "We're happy with how it's going. Nice and slow."

"Amen to that. Oh, I wanted to tell you. The other two guests at the inn are a handful. They ask for thirds at breakfast and wanted three fans in their room. They loved your shop, by the way, they visited yesterday morning. They keep asking Jimbo if he can teach them to communicate with plants. I didn't have the heart to tell them he was at Waffle House when he discovered his plant shamanism. Very romantic story involving hash browns and a Ficus. Still. He's going to give the guests a little tutorial this morning."

"That'll be entertaining," Liz said while scanning the room.

The hostess, a woman about our age wearing a name tag that said "Darlene" and sporting impressive bangs that defied both gravity and humidity, brought us water and asked if we wanted coffee. We both nodded. The vinyl seats squeaked as I shifted. Everything felt midcentury in here. The only thing missing was a smoking section.

"You've been here before?" I asked Liz.

She nodded, her eyes scanning the parking lot through the window. "They have excellent pie on Fridays. And a perfect view of the private roads that lead to Morning Glory Gardens."

"How far is it?"

"About a half mile down that dirt road." She pointed to a narrow, dusty road that disappeared into dense Florida scrub.

I fidgeted with the laminated menu, though I wasn't really reading it. "So you've been there. What's it like?"

"It's different," Liz said carefully. "I went there once with Luna from the coven, back when I was trying to source some herbs for the shop. I should've put two and two together earlier when the autopsy report mentioned a rare oleander. But I think my mind's foggy from the surgery still. Or it's perimenopause. Who knows! Anyway, Donna's not exactly friendly, but she knows her plants. The place gives me the creeps, though."

"More or less creepy than Larry the ghost building inspector?"

"Way more. Larry wants us to file the proper permits. Donna..." Liz sighed. "Let's just say she takes her plants very seriously. It makes sense that she's selling deadly oleander. Rumor has it that Donna's a witch, but she never participates in any of the town activities. And she's not a member of a coven, as far as I know."

Darlene appeared with two mugs of coffee. "Ready to order?"

"Coffee for now," Liz said. "We're waiting on someone." She gave me a meaningful look.

I caught on. We weren't actually waiting for anyone, but it gave us an excuse to linger and watch the road that led to Donna's.

"So what's our plan?" I asked once Darlene was out of earshot. "We can't waltz in and ask to see her rare, deadly oleander collection."

"Actually..." Liz's eyes sparkled with that saucy gleam I'd come to both love and fear. "I have an idea. But you're going to need to channel your inner actress."

I took a sip of coffee and waited for her to continue. This was going to be good.

"Before we go any further," I said, pulling a small notebook from my purse, "let's go over what we know. My brain is swimming with suspects."

Liz nodded and doctored her coffee with three sugar packets. "Good idea. Start with Sophia West."

"Right." I flipped open my notebook. "Sophia had an affair with Dominic. Dominic was into cocaine and forged art. Maybe fake jewelry, too. Who knows what kind of lowlifes that all attracted."

Liz and I looked at each other and grimaced. I shook my head and continued. "He took her grandmother's necklace under the pretense of authenticating it, then sold it. And according to that cute kid Luca at the party, she's been distraught and talking to someone about the necklace theft. But who? And why was she still with Dom after he did that to her? And why was she so friendly with Jack?"

"Suspicious, although maybe that was a one-off. Jack left the party pretty early, I noticed," Liz said. "Then there's her husband, Richard West."

"The developer? What's his motive?"

"Maybe he found out about the affair." Liz stirred her coffee thoughtfully. "Or maybe he discovered Dominic was running an art forgery ring. Although I don't know why he'd care about that — unless he bought art from Dom, thinking it was real."

"Good theory." I jotted that down. "Speaking of the forgeries, what about Thompson, the landlord? I wonder if he pressured Dominic into paying more rent. Or gave him a hard time about the fake art. Some sort of blackmail."

"Thompson owns that whole building, including the bistro next door. Amy — you know, our shadow-melding friend — said he's been raising rents like crazy. Maybe Dominic threatened to expose something about Thompson."

"Maybe. And then there's Jack," I said, writing his name with a question mark.

Liz leaned forward. "Now that's interesting. He was Dominic's pickleball partner, supposedly his friend. But he's been awfully cozy with Sophia. How did he meet Dom? What's their link?"

"And he's interested in Renee. Weird timing, if you ask me. Moves to town, meets Renee, man dies."

"He could want to throw suspicion off himself," Liz added.

I sighed and took another sip of coffee. "Don't forget Vanessa Reeves."

"Dominic's assistant slash secret fiancée." Liz made air quotes around the word fiancée. "Who opened the gallery the same day he died."

"And claimed to have evidence about witchcraft in his journal — which, by the way, didn't mention anything about witches until those last few paranoid entries. But that state of mind could've been the cocaine talking, too."

"Speaking of the journal..." Liz lowered her voice. "I made copies of the important pages before we returned it. I'll show you later."

I almost choked on my coffee. "Liz!"

"What? I'm dating the chief of police. I'm picking up investigative techniques." She grinned.

"You're incorrigible," I muttered, but couldn't help smiling. "Okay, last but not least: Donna Anderson, our mysterious greenhouse owner. What do we actually know about her?"

"Not much," Liz admitted. "She keeps to herself. Been here for years, doesn't really come into town much. I heard she does her shopping in Orlando. The local gardening witches respect her knowledge but say she's into some dark stuff."

Liz checked her watch. "The place opens at ten on weekdays. Donna runs a little farmer's market in the front. Mostly herbs and specialty plants for tourists. Also organic eggs. I've had the eggs, my neighbor buys them. Quite tasty. Rich in Omega 3, from the color of the yolk. Maybe we should pick up a few."

"A farmer's market at a poisonous plant greenhouse. Who would've thought? And no, I'll pass on the eggs if she's selling deadly plants."

"It's the perfect cover. Who's going to suspect anything weird about a place that sells organic basil and decorative succulents to tourists?" Liz pulled some cash from her wallet and tossed it on the table. "Come on. While everyone's distracted by the market, we can do some exploring."

We took Liz's Kia Soul, which she'd nicknamed the "Ghost Toaster" because of its boxy shape and color. As we bumped down the dirt road, my hands gripped the door handle. Either Liz had forgotten she'd recently had surgery, or she was auditioning for NASCAR. I turned down the radio, which was playing some sort of weird chanting music.

"Could you maybe slow down a little?" I asked as we hit another pothole.

"Sorry. I'm eager to get there. I haven't had any excitement since my gallbladder tried to kill me."

"I take it you're feeling better."

"Back in action, baby." She let out a little whoop and I snickered.

The greenhouse appeared around a bend, and I gasped. It was enormous, at least an acre under glass, with Victorian-style architecture that seemed wildly out of place in rural Florida. The metal framework had a greenish patina, and some of the glass panels were clouded with age. Vines crept up the exterior, their leaves pressing against the windows like tiny hands.

"Dang," I said. "It looks like Kew Gardens in England or something. It's right in the open. Wild."

"Yeah, if she's selling deadly plants, she's doing it under everyone's noses," Liz added.

A hand-painted sign reading "MORNING GLORY GARDENS FARM STAND" pointed to a tent set up near the parking area. About a dozen people milled around, examining baskets of herbs and flats of flowering plants. A woman in a floppy sun hat carefully selected eggs from a cooler. Meanwhile the greenhouse and its potentially menacing contents loomed large only a few feet away.

"Ready?" Liz asked, parking between a rusty pickup and a Subaru with a "Coexist" bumper sticker.

I nodded, though my stomach churned. "What's the plan?"

"Follow my lead." Liz grabbed her tie-dye reusable grocery bag and marched toward the farm stand tent with all the confidence in the world. I scurried to keep up.

A tall, older woman with steel-gray hair pulled into a severe bun stood behind a table of potted herbs. She wore cargo pants and a white, long-sleeved UV protection shirt despite the heat.

"Good morning! Are you Donna Anderson?" Liz chirped, way too cheerfully.

"Yes." The woman's tone was flat. Her eyes, flinty.

Liz beamed. "We're here about the composting workshop!"

I tried not to let my surprise show on my face.

The woman's eyes narrowed. "That's not until Sunday."

"Oh no!" Liz's hand flew to her mouth in an Oscar-worthy performance. "I could have sworn... Amelia, didn't you say it was Tuesday? I dragged you out of bed and everything!"

I caught on. "You definitely said it was today. I even brought my notebook to take notes about... uh, worm cultivation."

"Sorry." The woman began to turn away.

"Wait! Well, since we're here," Liz said to Donna, "could we maybe get a tour? My friend's new to gardening, and I've told her so much about your amazing greenhouse."

Donna's stern expression didn't change. "I don't do tours."

"Oh please?" Liz touched her midsection and winced. "I recently had surgery, and the doctor said gardening would be great therapy. Light activities only, you know? I'd love to show Amelia why I'm so passionate about plants. I'm trying to build my own greenhouse and was hoping we could get ideas."

I watched in amazement as Donna's face softened slightly. Then she shook her head. "Absolutely not. At least not today. I don't have time, and—"

She turned as if to say something to a young man restocking the tomato stand, but at that exact moment, there was a commotion at the egg cooler. My eyes almost popped out of my head when I saw the sign that said *EGGS — $15 a dozen.*

Fifteen bucks? How good were those eggs, anyway?

As I was mentally sputtering over the price, a woman in a floppy hat and large sunglasses had dropped her basket, sending eggs rolling everywhere. Two broke.

"Yikes," I whispered. Those things were like gold.

"Oh dear," the woman cried. "I'm so sorry! What should I do?"

The woman looked slightly familiar, but I thought that about a lot of people. Since moving to Cypress Grove, I felt like I'd met half of Florida.

Donna sighed. "Jason, help clean that up. You two ladies, wait here. I'll be right back."

The moment Donna turned away, Liz grabbed my arm and practically dragged me toward a side door of the greenhouse. I had to admit, the timing of that egg incident seemed suspiciously perfect.

"Liz," I whispered as she eased the door open, "please tell me you didn't arrange for someone to create a diversion."

She winked. "Let's just say some members of our coven are very committed to helping Renee. I called in a favor."

I followed her inside. The Florida air wrapped around us like a warm, earthy blanket, heavy with the scent of soil and growing things.

And something else, something sweet and deadly, like honey laced with undertones of rotting fruit. My stomach, which was empty except for the coffee, quivered.

Inside, the greenhouse was like something from a Victorian botanist's fever dream. Tendrils of mist curled around our feet, and condensation dripped from the glass panels overhead. The air was thick enough to chew, and every inhale felt like ingesting warm tea.

This was not a typical greenhouse. I recognized nothing. There were no snapdragons, no orchids, no spider plants.

I kept my arms pressed tightly against my sides, afraid to brush against anything. The plants here weren't your average garden-variety specimens. Strange flowers in impossible colors bloomed on twisted vines. What looked like a Venus flytrap the size of a dinner plate snapped lazily at a buzzing fly. Purple orchids seemed to pulse with their own inner light, and something that resembled Spanish moss glowed a faint blue.

"What the heck?" I whispered.

"Don't touch anything," Liz whispered, though she didn't need to tell me twice. "Some of these plants are seriously dangerous. Luna told me about a vine that can paralyze you with one brush of its leaves."

We crept down a narrow path between tables laden with exotic specimens. Labels written in Donna's precise handwriting identified each plant, though most names were in Latin and meant nothing to me. One particularly menacing-looking specimen was marked simply "Caution: Toxic."

"Over there." Liz pointed to a separate greenhouse room visible through a glass partition. "That's where she keeps the really dangerous stuff."

A sign on the door read "AUTHORIZED PERSONNEL ONLY" and below that, "PROTECTIVE EQUIPMENT REQUIRED BEYOND THIS POINT."

Something rustled in the foliage behind us, and I nearly jumped out of my skin. But it was a small fountain, its water feeding a collection of pitcher plants that definitely looked big enough to digest more than just insects. I squealed a little.

"Liz," I whispered, "I'm getting a really bad feeling about this place."

"Me too. But look." She gestured to a workbench near the restricted area. Several pairs of thick gardening gloves lay scattered across its surface, along with pruning shears and other tools.

I was about to respond when a plant to my left suddenly released a puff of iridescent spores. I held my breath and stepped back quickly, bumping into a shelf. A small terra cotta pot teetered, and I caught it right before it fell.

The moment my fingers touched the clay, the world shifted. I was still in the greenhouse, but it was night. Moonlight filtered through the glass, casting strange shadows. A figure moved among the plants, tall and willowy...

"Someone's coming!" Liz hissed, breaking my connection to the vision.

We heard footsteps approaching from the farm stand entrance. Heavy boots on the gravel path.

"Quick!" Liz grabbed my arm and pulled me behind a massive fern with fronds as long as my arm. Longer, even. The leaves were a deep burgundy color that I was pretty sure didn't exist in nature. What was going on here?

We crouched there, hardly daring to breathe, as the footsteps grew closer. Through gaps in the foliage, I could see Donna entering with a clipboard, followed by someone else.

"Where the hell are they?" she growled. "Did they come in here?"

From behind the colossal fern, I watched as Donna stomped past our hiding spot. Her boots crunched on scattered bits of potting soil and rocks, and I caught a whiff of something medicinal, like witch hazel mixed with vinegar.

"I told them to wait out front," Donna said to someone I couldn't see. "Nosy women. Always get them this time of year, thinking they can wander in. So entitled."

"The special order is ready," a male voice responded. It sounded young. Maybe it was Jason, her son. "But there's been another request. Two pounds this time."

"That's a large quantity," Donna said sharply. "Tell them the rare specimens take time. You can't rush these things. The molecular structure has to be right, or..." She lowered her voice to continue the conversation.

My thighs burned from crouching. A bead of sweat rolled down my back, and I was starting to feel light-headed from the thick air. That's when I noticed the burgundy fern's fronds slowly curling in our direction, as if they were fingers reaching for us.

What. The. Duck.

Liz noticed too, with a look of horror on her face. She grabbed my arm and pointed toward a sliver of daylight — a partially open door about fifteen feet away.

GO, she mouthed. RUN.

I shook my head. She pointed. The fern's frond tickled my arm. I opened my mouth to scream but Liz clapped her hand over my mouth.

We needed to scram. But we'd have to time this perfectly. The burgundy frond started to creep around my wrist. Holy crap. Liz plucked it away and the frond undulated in the air, as if chiding us.

My brain went into fight-or-flight mode. But I wasn't sure if I should fight the plant, or run. It had to be one or the other. Although I really hoped I didn't have to brawl with a plant today.

"...better double the next batch," Donna was saying, her voice moving toward the restricted area. "After what happened with the last client's results..."

The moment she and Jason disappeared behind the foggy glass partition, Liz and I crept out from behind the sentient fern. My sandal squished in something exceedingly spongy, and I decided not to look down because I didn't want to know what it was. I was breathing faster than when I was playing pickleball.

We'd almost reached the door when I heard Donna exclaim, "Did you leave this open?"

My heart nearly stopped.

"Run!" Liz whispered.

We burst out into the blinding Florida sunshine, booking it at full speed until we reached the Ghost Toaster. I jumped into the passenger seat as Liz fired up the engine. For some reason, the radio came on full blast, and Salt-N-Pepa's "Push It" blasted as we peeled out of the parking lot.

I caught a glimpse of Donna in my side mirror, standing in the greenhouse doorway with her hands on her hips.

"Holy cannoli," I yelled over the music. "What was all that?"

"A nightmare greenhouse of weirdness," Liz replied, taking

the curves of the dirt road way too fast while she turned down the volume knob on the radio. "But we learned something interesting."

"Yeah," I said, mopping sweat from my forehead. "Someone's ordering large quantities of her 'rare specimens.' And did you notice how specific she was about the molecular structure?"

"Exactly. Want to bet that deadly oleander was one of her special orders? Or that perhaps Donna is involved in some Colombian bam-bam?"

"What?"

"Cocaine," she yelled.

I nodded, then grabbed the dashboard as we hit a pothole. "Liz! You just had surgery!"

"Oops." She slowed down marginally. "Sorry. I'm worried she'll come after us."

"Well, I'm worried about whether we inhaled some lethal spores."

"Whatever. We're still alive, so I think we'll survive."

"Spoken like a Gen X-er," I said.

She slowed down and we pulled into the Sunny Side Up's parking lot, where my car sat baking in the late morning sun. The diner's neon sign still blinked uncertainly, and the place was even more packed than before, with a line out the door.

Liz drummed her fingers on the steering wheel. "All very interesting. Super interesting." She looked at the front of the diner. "You know who we need to talk to now? Thompson."

"The building's landlord? Because of my vision in Dom's office?"

She turned in my direction. "Yeah. Remember how Sophia said he knew about Dominic's art schemes? The fake paintings coming in, real ones going out? Plus, he owns that whole building complex. The gallery, the bistro, everything. If Dominic was into shady stuff, Thompson might have known. Or something."

I thought back to that vision, how angry Dominic had been when Sophia mentioned Thompson watching his late-night deliveries. How he'd accused Thompson of blackmail. "He was pressuring Dominic about the rent," I said slowly. "But maybe there was more to it than that."

"Speaking of pressure," Liz said, checking her phone, "Chris just texted. We're taking Winston to that new dog park later." She grinned. "Still trying to determine if he's secretly a werewolf. Chris, that is. Winston isn't. Winston's a good boy."

"This again?" I laughed. There were rumors around town that Chris Wolf was a werewolf. I'd never believed the gossip, feeling that it was too on-the-nose. A werewolf with the last name of Wolf who owned a husky named Winston. What were the odds?

"What's the evidence this time?" I asked. "Other than his love for the coyote sanctuary?"

"He howls in his sleep sometimes. And he gets really grumpy around the full moon."

"That could be the cop thing. Or a man thing."

"True. But he's very protective of his territory."

"Again, probably the cop thing."

We both chuckled, but Liz was already dialing her phone. "Let me call Amy at the bistro about Thompson. She's plugged in to everything that goes on in that building."

While Liz made the call, I watched a young family pile out of a minivan with South Carolina plates, the kids racing each other to the diner's entrance. Normal Florida stuff. Hard to believe we'd fled from a greenhouse full of murderous plants only a few minutes ago. What was that fern, anyway? A shiver went through me at the memory of it trying to curl around my wrist.

"Got it," Liz said, ending the call. "Okay. Thompson's office is around the back of the gallery building. There's a separate entrance by the parking lot. Amy says he's usually there on weekday mornings, doing paperwork." She paused. "She also says he's kind of a grump, but he tips well at the bistro."

"Sounds promising. At least he's not growing deadly plants."

"That we know of." Liz checked the time. "I should go. Chris gets anxious if Winston misses his scheduled play date. The dog, I mean. Though honestly, sometimes I wonder about Chris too."

I snorted as I reached for the door handle. "Go. Have fun with your maybe-werewolf boyfriend and his definitely-not-werewolf dog. I'll check out Thompson's office and text you later."

When I climbed out, she screeched off.

I'd barely taken three steps toward my car when Liz returned. She rolled down her window, looking deadly serious. Had I left something in her car?

"Do werewolves need flea and tick prevention?" she asked.

I blinked. "What?"

"Chris keeps scratching behind his ear. Like a dog. And he's been really worried about ticks lately. Says they're bad this year."

"Go to the dog park," I said firmly.

She sighed dramatically. "Fine. But if he starts chasing squirrels, I'm calling you."

Shaking my head, I watched Liz drive away in the Ghost Toaster, already mentally prepping myself for what I might discover in Thompson's office. At least this time, I was pretty sure there wouldn't be any carnivorous plants.

Pretty sure.

Sixteen

I pulled into the backlot of the gallery building and parked between a dumpster that smelled vaguely of coffee grounds and a brick wall covered in sloppy graffiti.

While the gallery was silent and closed, the bistro's lunch line spilled out onto the street, all designer sunglasses and carefully curated outfits. Through the windows, I could see servers balancing plates of avocado toast and carrying Mason jars filled with something that was probably called a "craft mimosa."

The brick building itself was old Florida. Probably turn of the century, with tall windows, detailed crown molding, and a few architectural flourishes that spoke of grander days. Now it was hipster heaven, complete with a chalkboard sign advertising oat milk lattes.

I made my way to the back door, following Amy's directions. The rear of the building was less polished than the front, with exposed brick and metal stairs leading to various offices and possibly apartments. A faded door with peeling paint had THOMPSON HOLDINGS stenciled across its frosted glass window. Very film noir. I half expected to hear a saxophone playing somewhere.

I knocked.

"It's open," a man's gruff voice called from inside.

The door creaked as I stepped into a space that seemed frozen in time. The office was lined with dark wood paneling and illuminated by green banker's lamps. A huge mahogany desk dominated the room. Behind it sat a man. Thompson, I guessed. He looked exactly like the kind of person who belonged in this office.

Filing cabinets lined one wall. Venetian blinds cast sunlight stripes across everything, and a ceiling fan spun lazily overhead, its shadow playing across scattered papers and leather-bound ledgers. The air smelled of old books, dust, and something else. Aftershave. Definitely Old Spice. A scent that had been around for decades, like the wearer.

A collection of vintage postcards was tacked to a corkboard, their edges curled with age, showing scenes from a Cypress Grove that didn't exist anymore. In one corner, an ancient radio sat atop a stack of yellowing newspapers.

Thompson was a big man, probably in his sixties, with the kind of face that suggested this wasn't his second, third, or even fourth rodeo. His white shirt had the sleeves rolled up, revealing forearms decorated with faded tattoos. A small electric fan oscillated on a filing cabinet, fighting a losing battle with the Florida heat.

I felt underdressed in my jeans, T-shirt, and sneakers. I felt like I should be wearing a tweed suit, red lipstick, and high heels. Maybe a hat. I almost expected him to call me a "dame."

This whole scene was unusual, even considering that an hour ago I'd almost been strangled by a fern.

"Ms. Matthews," he said, not looking up from whatever he was writing. "I wondered when you'd show up."

I gaped, thrown off balance. "You know who I am?"

He finally looked up, his eyes shrewd but not unkind. "I make it my business to know everyone's business in my properties. That includes Pickled. I own that building, in case you didn't know, so I'm aware of recent events. I'm Reese Thompson."

Well. This seemed like important news, that he owned Pickled.

He gestured to a wooden chair that had seen some things over the decades. "Have a seat. My research tells me that since you only recently inherited the inn from Shirley — rest her soul, she was a lovely woman, we had lunch together every few months — you're not looking for a studio to rent."

Something about his demeanor reminded me of my favorite old movie characters — those world-weary types who'd seen enough to be cynical but retained a hidden soft spot for justice. I settled into the chair, which was surprisingly comfortable. The fact that he knew my aunt made me like the guy a little. But could I trust him?

I looked to my right and my eyes peeled open. An elderly Shih Tzu with a gray muzzle was curled up in a pink fluffy bed beside his desk.

The dog's chin rested on tiny paws, and a rhinestone collar sparkled at its neck. A crystal water bowl with "Princess" etched on it sat nearby. The dog opened one eye to assess me, decided I wasn't worth moving for, and went back to sleep with a tiny wheezing snore.

Thompson caught me staring, and his stern expression softened slightly. "That's Princess. She's fifteen. Ex-wife's dog, but Princess decided to stay with me in the divorce. Guess she preferred bourbon to wine spritzers."

He reached down to gently scratch behind her ear, his large, tattooed hand comically massive next to her tiny head. Princess' fluffy tail gave two lazy thumps against her bed, but she didn't bother opening her eyes.

"I'm interested in Dominic Harper," I said directly. No point in beating around the bush with someone like this guy.

"Aren't we all?" He opened a drawer and pulled out a cut-crystal tumbler and a bottle of something amber. "Drink?"

"It's not noon yet." I paused. "Well, okay."

"That's the spirit." He poured two glasses of what looked like bourbon and handed me one. "What do you want to know?"

I took a sip and nearly sputtered the liquid onto the desk. It was too early for such a strong drink, but when in Rome. "You knew about his art forgery operation."

It wasn't a question, but he answered anyway. ""Of course I did. Hard to miss when you're seeing giant crates coming in through the back loading dock at 2 AM several times a week. Expensive artwork being unloaded by groups of men I'd never seen before, not Dom's regular staff. They'd always park their unmarked vans to block the security cameras' view. But my hidden backup cameras caught everything."

He took a sip. "Odd how the pieces they brought in at night never seemed to match what was on display the next day. And the volume, it was way more art moving through than any small gallery in Cypress Grove could legitimately be selling. Do you know how many people buy art in that joint?"

I shook my head.

"Other than the tourists buying the cheap eight-by-ten prints? None. I've never seen anyone leave that place during the daytime with a large, framed piece. Ever. Don't you think that's odd?"

It sounded like it, but I knew nothing about the inner workings of art businesses. "Did you confront him about it?"

Thompson's laugh was dry as his bourbon. "Confront? No. I merely adjusted his rent to reflect the, shall we say, risk factor of his business model." He studied me for a moment. "But that's not really what you want to know, is it?"

I leaned forward slightly. "What did you notice about Dominic's friends and acquaintances?"

His eyebrows rose slightly. "Ah. Now we're getting somewhere." He swirled his drink thoughtfully. "That Jack character, the one who runs around town grinning with those white teeth like he's a Sears catalog model, started showing up in the past month or so, during those late-night meetings. Always hanging around, watching. One time I happened to be here and found Jack waiting for Dom outside. Claimed he was meeting Dom about some investment opportunity, but I never saw any actual business happening."

"You don't sound convinced."

"Ms. Matthews, I've been around long enough to know when someone's keeping tabs on someone else. Jack wasn't there for investments." He paused, then added, "And he wasn't the only one watching Dominic."

"Vanessa?"

Thompson nodded. "That girl was obsessed. She'd sit in her car across the street for hours after the gallery closed, watching his office window. Even followed him a few times." He took another sip. "Got it all on camera. Dom, of course, was enthralled with her." Thompson held his hands in front of his chest, as if he was cradling breasts.

I nearly choked on my bourbon. "Camera?"

"Of course. You think I'd own a building complex like this without security cameras?" He gestured to a monitor partially hidden behind a potted palm tree. "Had them installed last year after noticing some irregular activities."

"The art forgeries?"

"Among other things. Most of them having nothing to do with Dom." Thompson set down his glass and leaned back in his chair. "I've been cooperating with the FDLE investigator. Agent Martinez. Nice woman. She's particularly interested in those late-night meetings."

My stomach tightened. "FDLE. Yeah, they took over the case from the locals."

His eyes fixed on me. "They're casting a wide net. Looking into everyone connected to Dominic's death, including your friend Renee."

I set my glass down carefully. "Why Renee? How do you know about her?"

"She's involved in one of the largest covens in town. I've met her a few times, the ex-wife used to take some artsy-fartsy crafting class from her. Agent Martinez seems very interested in Renee." He nodded at the computer on his desk. "I gave them all my security footage, but I kept copies. I always keep copies."

The bourbon sat heavy in my stomach. Was he lying?

"Mr. Thompson," I started, but he cut me off.

"Just Thompson. And before you ask. Yes, I've seen some interesting things on those tapes. Things that might help your friend. Or hurt her." He shrugged, right as a sliver of light through the blinds hit his desk. "Depends on what else turns up in the investigation."

I studied him, wondering how much I could actually trust. After all, he'd known about Dominic's illegal activities and done nothing except raise the rent. That didn't exactly scream "upstanding citizen."

Despite the strangeness of the situation, I felt an odd sense of calm settling over me. Maybe it was the way time seemed to move differently in here, like the office existed in its own dimension where modern problems couldn't quite reach.

Or maybe it was Thompson himself. There was something reassuring about his no-nonsense demeanor, like finding an adult who actually had their stuff together in a world full of chaos. The gentle whirring of the fan and the filtered sunlight made everything feel slightly dreamy, like I was in an old movie where problems always got solved by the final scene.

"You seem skeptical, Ms. Matthews." Thompson's eyes crinkled with something like amusement.

"Amelia. Just Amelia. Can you blame me? For all I know, you were part of Dominic's operation."

"Ah." He reached for his keyboard. "I had a feeling you might need some convincing. Give me a moment."

A soft jingling caught my attention as Princess, who had apparently decided this was worth waking up for, slowly raised herself from her bed. She waddled over to my chair, her long hair swaying like a dust mop, and placed one tiny paw on my shoe.

The gesture was so delicate, so incongruous with everything else about this office, that I couldn't help but grin.

"She's got a good sense about people," Thompson said, watching as Princess attempted to climb into my lap, her arthritic back legs scrambling until I gave her a boost. "Usually sleeps through most of my meetings. Except when she thinks someone needs a friend."

He pulled a treat from his desk drawer — the dog treats were next to the bourbon — and handed it to me. "She likes to be scratched right behind her left ear while she eats those."

As I fed Princess her treat and found the sweet spot behind her ear, I felt my racing thoughts begin to slow. Something about petting this tiny, elderly dog while sitting in this time capsule of an office made everything feel more manageable. Thompson clicked and typed for about a minute and the dog appeared to want to get down.

I set her on the floor and she ambled back to her bed. I straightened my spine and took another sip, my eyes on Thompson the entire time.

The sleek monitor on his desk seemed out of place among the vintage office decor. He swiveled it toward me, and I nearly dropped my glass from what I saw on the screen.

"Before we go further," he said, "let's address the elephant in the room."

The screen showed Liz and me in our amateur cat burglar glory, tiptoeing through the gallery. I tried not to register any emotion on my face as I watched Amy literally walk through a wall. But when I saw my own shocked face on the video, I winced.

I looked like that yellow Pokemon character that my daughter loved when she was a kid.

"Oh crap," I whispered.

"Interesting technique," Thompson said dryly. "I had to upgrade my security system last year to catch shadow melding on camera. Cost me an arm and a leg." He leaned back in his chair. "Don't worry, I didn't show this to the police. Partly because I like you, and partly because..." He gestured at Amy's ghostly form on screen. "Try explaining that. No, don't want this on any official records."

I cracked a smile, and so did Thompson.

"About that. I can explain-"

"Look, Ms. Matthews, I've been a landlord in Cypress Grove for twenty years. I may not have powers, but I know enough to install cameras that can see through invisibility spells. Cost me a fortune, but it's necessary. Plus I get an insurance discount." He clicked through several files. "But that's not what concerns me right now."

"The FDLE is focused on the murder," Thompson said. "But while they're building their case, things are still going on in the gallery. Art is coming and going. Mostly, I don't want any trouble in my buildings. Don't want shady stuff happening, and I wish I'd never rented to Dominic. I was planning on not renewing his lease when it came due in a few months. I'm happy to have your help in this matter."

"You are? Why me?" I asked.

"Because you notice things others miss. I've heard about the cases you've solved. I'm familiar with your reputation and your powers." He pulled out a file. "And because I've been working with the FBI's Art Crime Team as a confidential informant. They're close to breaking up the forgery ring, but this murder has complicated everything."

I watched the screen as various clips played. There were furtive meetings between people I didn't recognize, late-night exchanges, and suspicious packages changing hands. The clips were from a month ago, and Dom was in every one.

"The FDLE is building their case about the murder," Thompson continued. "Meanwhile, the FBI's Art Crime Team is focused on breaking up the forgery ring. But that's the problem with law enforcement. Every agency stays in their lane, guards their own cases. FDLE won't step on FBI toes, FBI won't interfere with a state homicide investigation. Critical connections get missed because nobody wants to share intel." He looked at me meaningfully. "Nobody except maybe you."

How did he know all this? And why did he think it was important information for me to have? "And you're telling and showing me everything because...?"

"Because somebody in this town killed Dominic Harper, and they're still walking around free, probably thinking they've outsmarted the cops." He smiled grimly. "So far, they are."

"Who do you think did it?" I asked, swirling the last of my bourbon.

Thompson leaned back, the leather of his chair creaking. "If I were a betting man? I'd put money on Sophia West's husband. I've known him for years, before he married Sophia. He doesn't suffer fools lightly. Then again..." He paused. "Vanessa is an interesting character."

My pulse quickened. "You think she killed him? Or set him up?"

"Depends on whether she found out about Dom and Sophia. People do crazy things for love. Or money. Or both." He clicked through more footage. "I shared my suspicions with the FDLE, but they seem more interested in your friend Renee and her coven."

"But why? She'd never met Dominic before."

"She hadn't?"

I was shaking my head as Thompson tapped a few keys. "This was a week before Dominic died."

The video timestamp read 2:47 AM. On screen, a figure I recognized as Renee moved through the frame, holding what looked like a burning sage stick. She waved the smoking herb bundle in a figure eight. The camera angle switched, showing her kneeling, hands raised toward the building. The image quality wasn't great, but there was definitely an eerie glow around her hands.

"Oh no," I muttered. Princess' head popped up at my tone, her tiny ears perking forward.

"Gets better." Thompson switched to another angle. The glow from Renee's hands intensified, and even on the grainy footage, I could see her lips moving. She touched the wall of the building, right near Dominic's gallery window, and a flash of light briefly whited out the camera. "Agent Martinez was particularly interested in this part."

I felt sick. I knew Renee did protection and cleansing rituals. All senior coven members did. But this looked bad. Really bad. To anyone who didn't understand magic, it would appear as though she was cursing the building. Cursing Dominic, even. That didn't link her to the poison that killed him, of course, but it was deeply suspicious.

"The FDLE has experts who analyze spells like this. Of course, the agency denies the existence of those experts, but I'm familiar with them," Thompson said quietly. "I've got cameras all over this building and a few others, but Pickled…"

He shook his head. "Different system there. Not as sophisticated. And I don't put cameras in bathrooms or locker rooms. I'm an SOB, but I'm not a pervert."

"Good to know," I murmured, and he smirked.

"Anyway, the FDLE is calling Renee's actions 'consistent with hostile intent.' " He leaned back, watching my face. "Care to explain why your friend was casting spells at my building in the middle of the night?"

My mind raced. I'd been with Renee that afternoon, before Dominic died. She hadn't mentioned anything about late-night rituals. "I can't," I admitted. "But I know Renee. Whatever this was, there has to be an explanation."

"I hope you're right." Thompson turned the monitor back to face him. "Because right now, the FDLE is building a case that your friend magically cursed Dominic Harper before he died under mysterious circumstances. And given the fact that she's also likely familiar with poisonous herbs and spells… let's just say the authorities can't prosecute magic, but they can prosecute poisoning."

I stared at the blank screen, my bourbon forgotten. I needed to talk to Renee.

"How do you know all this about law enforcement?" I asked, once again suspicious. "How do you have such good sources?"

Thompson was quiet for a second, then said, "I was a cop. Tampa PD. Nineteen years." His voice had gotten softer, almost contemplative. "Left under what you might call complicated circumstances. But I kept some connections. Old habits die hard."

"What kind of complicated circumstances?"

He smiled, but it didn't reach his eyes. "The kind that make a man decide to become a landlord in a town full of witches instead." He glanced to his left, at the blank, wood paneled wall. "Sometimes the people you think are guilty aren't, and the ones you never suspect are the worst criminals of all."

"Yikes," I whispered, taking a long slug of my drink.

"Yikes is right. You need to be careful out there." He pointed a pen at my glass. "Want a refresh?"

I reached into my purse and pulled out my card. Thompson took it, then handed me one of his.

"No. Thanks, though, Mr. Thompson. I've gotta go. Don't hesitate to call me if you think of anything else. You've been a big help."

A big help in confusing me even more.

Seventeen

I stumbled out of Thompson's office into the bright Florida sunshine, my head spinning from both bourbon and investigative details. The temperature had climbed while I'd been in that time capsule of an office, and the lunch brunch crowd had only grown larger. My mouth felt like sandpaper. Stinky sandpaper.

I rounded the corner to the bistro's to-go counter, ready to embrace my basic destiny and order something with oat milk and too many syllables, when I spotted Amy at the cash register. Even in the middle of the day, she had a slight shimmer around her edges that marked her as not-quite-corporeal.

"Amy! Hey!" I waved. "How's it going?"

"Not bad. You?" She beamed. "Everything cool after the events of the other night?"

"Well, not exactly. No, they're not cool at all. In fact, they're quite uncool." I grimaced.

She must have sensed my anxiety, because she immediately told another server that she was taking five. I followed her out a side door and into the hallway, where we'd broken into the gallery the other night.

"Renee's in trouble," I blurted, the words tumbling out. "Thompson showed me security footage of her doing some kind of ritual right outside Dominic's gallery window, and the FDLE has these supposed magical forensics experts who say it was hostile intent, and—"

Amy's laughter cut me off. Not a polite chuckle, but a full-on guffaw that echoed in the hall.

"Oh honey," she wiped at her eyes, her southern accent thick, "is that what this is about? The ritual last week?" She was still chuckling. "I'm the one who called her here."

I blinked. "Huh?"

"We had a server a while back. He died in a paddleboard accident in Clearwater a few months ago."

I nodded slowly, trying to follow. "Sorry about your friend. But what does he have to do with Renee?"

She waved me off. "I didn't know him well, he worked weekends. But he had some unfinished business with the tip-sharing system. He's been haunting the place, knocking over mimosa trays, changing orders in the POS system, generally making everyone's life miserable. I asked Renee to do a cleansing ritual because she's great at those."

Amy paused and grinned. "But she did it at night so the regular customers wouldn't freak out. I didn't want to attract the attention of the manager or anyone at the gallery."

I slumped against the wall, relief making my knees weak. "She wasn't cursing Dominic?"

"Cursing? Please. She was trying to convince Joey that the great beyond was better than hanging around making the servers' lives miserable. That flash of light? That was Joey finally moving on. Although now that I think about it, it probably did look pretty sketchy on camera."

I closed my eyes, thinking about how things appeared to outsiders versus the reality of life in Cypress Grove. To Thompson and the FDLE, they'd seen a witch performing mysterious rituals in the dark. To us, it was simply another weekday.

"Well, that's a relief, I guess." I sighed, and we started to walk back toward the bistro. "Sorry to pull you away from work."

"No problem. You want anything from the kitchen?"

"A sweet tea would be amazing. And maybe something with protein to soak up that bourbon."

"The breakfast burrito is good," Amy offered as we started to walk back to the bistro. "Joey's not around to mess with the orders anymore. I'll get you one. Chorizo, or no?"

"Make it two. With chorizo. Spicy." Oliver loved Mexican food, and he and his calm, sexy demeanor were exactly what I needed right now. Along with the burrito.

We walked back into the restaurant, and I had to blink at the sudden shift from bland, white hallway to Instagram-ready interior. This place really was lovely, with exposed brick walls dripping with pothos plants, geometric light fixtures casting artful shadows, and wooden tables that probably had origin stories about reclaimed barn wood.

The shadows around Amy seemed to pulse with her laughter, creating rippling patterns on the walls that the customers probably assumed were from the hanging plants. A toddler at a nearby table pointed at the effect with sticky fingers, but his mom was too busy photographing her eggs benedict to notice.

"Your shadow's showing," I murmured.

"Let it," she grinned. "The kids think it's some kind of avant-garde light installation. Last week someone tagged us in a reel about our innovative ambient lighting design." She rolled her eyes, but I could tell she was pleased with herself.

The shadows danced around her feet as she led the way to the counter.

I smiled and shook my head. This place, man. Wild.

I went over to Oliver's with the burritos, unannounced. When I pulled into his driveway, my mood improved at the sight of him on his front porch.

He sat in one of two white Adirondack chairs, a stack of

papers on his lap, and a giant glass of iced coffee on the table between the chairs. His glasses had slipped down his nose in that adorably professorial way that always made me smile. He needed a haircut, but even a messy mop of hair looked good on him.

Oliver glanced up as I climbed out of the car with the burrito bag.

"Well, this is a nice surprise," he called out. "I didn't think I'd get a chance to see you today."

"I brought sustenance." I held up the paper bag. "Chorizo brunch burritos from Sage and Salt. And hoo boy, do I have some updates for you."

"Updates that require emergency burritos?" His eyes sparkled. "Must be serious."

A grin spread on his face as he moved his papers off the table and shoved them into a leather messenger bag. "Pull up a chair, Detective Matthews."

I settled into the empty Adirondack chair, kicking off my sandals and enjoying the feel of the wooden slats under my feet. The porch was shaded by a large, squat palm tree.

"Your inn guests survive without you this morning?" he asked, reaching for the bag.

"Jimbo's giving them a plant workshop. I suspect they're all sitting in a circle around a potted Ficus, trying to sense its aura."

Oliver laughed and gestured to the stack of papers. "Meanwhile, I'm drowning in summer school essays on the paranormal history of Florida. Half of them think the Skunk Ape is behind every mysterious occurrence in the state. One student wrote an entire paper suggesting the Fountain of Youth was actually a primitive hot tub."

I snorted, pulling out our wrapped burritos. "If only it were that simple. Though honestly, after what I saw this morning, a Skunk Ape would be refreshingly straightforward. Although, wait. What is a Skunk Ape?"

"Florida's version of a Bigfoot." He unwrapped his burrito. "This looks delicious. Thanks. What happened this morning?"

"What didn't happen, is more like it?"

As we ate, I gave him the CliffsNotes version of my morning, from the greenhouse adventure with its touchy ferns to my bourbon-enhanced chat with Thompson.

"What?" Oliver interrupted, his burrito halfway to his mouth. "The fern tried to grab you?"

"Tried? It practically felt me up." I demonstrated with my hands. "The fronds were all..." I wiggled my fingers menacingly.

"And this was before or after the morning bourbon?"

"Ha ha. The bourbon came after the sentient plant."

He chuckled and reached over to brush a strand of hair from my face. The gesture was so tender, so naturally affectionate, that my heart did a little flip.

"You know," he said softly, "most people's weekday plans involve going to work and maybe watching a little TV."

"Where's the fun in that?"

My phone buzzed, interrupting the moment. I apologized to Oliver as he was taking a giant bite of the burrito. Hopefully there was nothing serious happening at the inn, because I wanted to relax and rest here with Oliver for a couple of hours. Jimbo was usually pretty good about handling any issues — he'd worked at the inn for years and had been hired by my aunt.

"Oh, it's Thompson," I murmured when I saw the number. I stood up and began to pace on the porch as I read the message.

> After you left, I was inspired to go through last week's videos again. Found something interesting in the footage from last night. You need to see this.

I tapped the attached video and pressed play.

Eighteen

The video on my phone was dark and grainy, but there was no mistaking what I was looking at: Jack and Vanessa. The image blew apart every half-baked theory I had about Dominic's death, and I had to hand Oliver the phone.

"We need to go inside. I can't focus out here," I said.

Oliver, being the organized and kind person that he is, scooped up everything and toted it indoors to the dining room table — a long, sprawling thing that held books and files on one end. We sat at the other, clear end and pulled chairs close together.

"Okay, let's see what's going on here," he said, cradling the phone horizontally in his hands.

They were the only two figures in Thompson's security footage. They were in the gallery after hours, heads close together, hands gesturing emphatically. In one clip, Jack pulled Vanessa into an embrace that definitely wasn't platonic.

"Stop it right there," I said, jabbing my finger at my phone screen. "That's not a business meeting."

"Uh, no. That looks like something *very* private." Oliver let out a chuckle.

The security footage showed Jack and Vanessa in the darkened gallery. His hand lingered on her forearm while she leaned into him and kissed his neck. My stomach tightened as we scrolled through more clips Thompson had sent.

"There's at least four meetings like this," I said. "Always after hours, always the two of them. And look at this one. They're fighting about something."

Oliver shifted closer, his shoulder warm against mine as he studied the video. His reading glasses slid down his nose, and I resisted the urge to push them back up. We watched the videos a second time, then a third, as the reality dawned on me.

"At the pickleball court, Jack pretended to be shocked when Vanessa said she was Dominic's fiancée, as if he didn't know her." I licked my lips. "That was a lie. It was all a lie."

"You need to show this to Liz, and the cops," he said. "And while you do that, let me dig around online. Sometimes public records tell us more than security footage."

"Don't you think the police have done that? Look into everyone's background?"

Oliver shrugged. "Yes, probably. But just in case, we should also check."

I nodded and looked at the burritos, which were lying on the table half-eaten. So much for a relaxing lunch.

I found Liz arranging crystals at the Astral Attic. Fortunately, there were no customers. She took one look at my face and flipped the OPEN sign to CLOSED.

"Whatever it is, I'm guessing it can't wait," she said, locking the front door.

We huddled behind the counter, watching clip after clip sent by Thompson. Liz gripped my arm when we got to the footage of Jack pulling Vanessa into an embrace.

"I knew it," she whispered. "I knew something was off about him pursuing Renee. The timing felt wrong."

"But why?" I rewound the clip. "Why pretend to be interested in Renee if he's involved with Vanessa?"

My phone rang. It was Oliver.

"Put him on speaker," Liz said.

Oliver's voice filled the quiet shop. "I did a search in all civil records in Florida. Marriage license from three years ago in Broward County for Jack Spencer and Vanessa Mitchell. They also jointly own a house in Deerfield Beach."

"What?" Liz and I both yelped in tandem.

The truth stole my breath. Not because it was shocking, but because it made perfect sense.

"They're married," I said. "Everything at the club that day was fake. Vanessa claiming to be Dominic's fiancée, her claiming that our coven was out to get Dom..."

"She was acting," Liz finished. "Creating a scene to distract everyone."

"Maybe Jack wanted to date Renee to throw us off further." The pieces clicked faster now. "Make it impossible for anyone to connect him to Vanessa."

"The real question," Oliver said through the phone, "is what they're hiding that's worth all this deception."

I thought of my vision in the gallery, of Dominic and Sophia discussing forged artwork. Of all the late-night deliveries Thompson had mentioned. Of toxic plants and secret meetings.

"Dom wasn't murdered by the mafia," I blurted. "Or by witches. He was killed by the people he trusted the most."

After I ended the call with Oliver, Liz gestured toward the back of the store. "I need tea. You need tea. We both need tea."

"Is this a real need for caffeine, or are you stress brewing?" I called after her.

"Both! Let's stay away from the window so tourists won't see us and bang on the door."

I followed her, my sandals slapping against the wood floor. The Lounge was cozy as always. A pan flute melody played softly from hidden speakers, totally opposite of my anxious mood. The news that Jack and Vanessa were married made so much sense, and yet, it opened up many new and evil possibilities.

"I can't believe we didn't think of this," Liz muttered while measuring loose tea into a strainer. "Jack and Vanessa. Married. Playing us all like a bunch of crystal singing bowls."

"But what did they want with Renee, specifically?" The thought made my stomach churn. "What kind of people pretend to be strangers, just to set someone up?"

"Murderous people," Liz said grimly. She poured hot water over the tea leaves, and the spicy scent of chai filled the air. "The question is why? What's their angle? Why Renee? Why Jack?"

I slumped into my favorite armchair, the purple velvet one. "Well, we know Dominic was running an art forgery ring. Obviously Jack and Vanessa were in on it. It's totally possible they all know each other from years past. Or from the art world. Birds of a feather, and all that."

"And what, it went bad?" Liz handed me a steaming mug decorated with phases of the moon.

"Or they wanted to take over the operation." I wrapped my hands around the warm ceramic, letting its heat ground me. "Thompson said pieces are still leaving the gallery, even after Dom's death."

My phone buzzed again. Oliver.

"Hold that thought," I told Liz, answering quickly. "Hey, what's up?"

"Check your email," he said, sounding slightly winded, like he was walking fast. I heard the slam of a car door. "I did some digging into Jack and Vanessa's background. You're not going to believe what I found. I have to run. My summer session students are waiting. But text me later after you've digested the newspaper articles. Love you."

He hung up before I could respond.

I stared at my phone, my heart doing a strange little *thump thump thump* in my chest. Did Oliver say...

Love you.

He'd never said those words before. We'd been dating and exclusive for months, but neither of us had crossed that particular verbal threshold.

And he'd dropped it so casually, like it wasn't a major relationship milestone. Like he hadn't shifted my entire emotional universe while I was in the middle of investigating a murder.

A warm, fizzy feeling spread through me, making my toes tingle. Part of me wanted to jump up and down like a teenager, but I was a grown woman sitting in a metaphysical shop, drinking chai, and supposedly focusing on solving a crime. But, was I ready for this next step in our relationship?

"What did Oliver say?" Liz asked, settling into the chair across from me with her own cup of chai. "You've got a weird look on your face. Are you having a hot flash?"

"Yeah, maybe," I said slowly. "Oh, uh, Oliver found something about Jack and Vanessa. Said it was important and sent some articles. Lemme look."

I balanced my mug on the arm of the chair and pulled up my email, grateful for the distraction. Whatever Oliver had discovered about our mysterious married couple would help me focus on the case instead of replaying those two little words in my head.

The email loaded, and my jaw dropped. "Oh duck," I whispered, the warm fuzzies from Oliver's declaration instantly replaced by a cold wave of dread. "This changes everything. Ho. Lee. Crap."

"What is it?"

I continued to read silently, shaking my head.

"Tell me," Liz practically shrieked.

I handed her the phone. "Not only do Jack and Vanessa have several aliases, but they've committed other crimes in towns with metaphysical communities. Oliver did a statewide criminal record search and found an arrest report with their fake names. Then he poked around a bit more and discovered a bunch of newspaper articles. Sedona. Salem. St. Augustine."

"And now Cypress Grove," she said grimly.

SEDONA CITIZEN-TIMES
Art Gallery Heist Charges Dropped; Local Psychics Maintain Innocence
By Maria Santiago

SEDONA, Arizona. — Charges were dismissed Monday against Jonathan and Victoria Reed in connection with the theft of $2.3 million in Native American artifacts from Red Rock Gallery, leaving questions unanswered and the local metaphysical community reeling from months of accusations and suspicion.

The Reeds, who operated a spiritual healing center near the gallery, were arrested in January after several valuable pieces disappeared from the prestigious downtown gallery. Initial police reports suggested involvement from local psychics who had reportedly performed ceremonies near the building.

"This case has torn apart our community," said Sarah Whitehawk, president of the Sedona Metaphysical Alliance. "Many of our members lost clients and faced harassment due to false accusations and rumors. Some practitioners had to close their businesses."

The case against the Reeds collapsed when their attorneys, from prominent Phoenix law firm Davidson & Mitchell, successfully argued that key evidence was obtained without proper warrants. Security footage showing suspicious activity was also ruled inadmissible due to chain of custody issues.

Det. James Martinez, spokesman for the Sedona Police Department, expressed frustration with the outcome. "We believe valuable artifacts are still missing, and someone knows where they are. This investigation remains open."

Former gallery employee Thomas Running Horse said the Reeds began frequenting the gallery six months before the thefts. "They claimed to be interested in the spiritual significance of our Native pieces. They gained everyone's trust."

Sources close to the investigation, speaking on condition of anonymity, said the Reeds disappeared shortly after their release, leaving behind an empty rental property and numerous unpaid bills.

Similar incidents have been reported at galleries in other metaphysical tourist destinations, though no direct connections have been established.

The gallery's insurance company has filed civil suits against multiple parties. Red Rock Gallery owner Matthew Scott declined to comment, citing ongoing litigation.

"The real tragedy here," Whitehawk added, "is that while everyone was busy accusing legitimate spiritual practitioners, the actual perpetrators walked away."

A separate FBI investigation into the missing artifacts remains active.

SALEM EVENING NEWS
Historic Salem Art Theft Investigation Ends with Dropped Charges
By Tamara Kornfeld/The Associated Press

SALEM, Mass. (AP) — Prosecutors have dropped charges against Benjamin and Rose Winters in the theft of several 18th-century portraits and artifacts from the Essex Maritime Gallery, citing insufficient evidence and procedural issues.

The Winters, who ran a "haunted history" walking tour company, were arrested after $1.8 million in colonial-era artwork vanished from the gallery during Salem's peak tourist season. Local witches and psychics initially faced scrutiny when ceremonial herbs were found near broken display cases.

"They played on our town's history," said Morgan Ravens, owner of The Crystal Cauldron shop. "While police were interrogating legitimate practitioners about 'suspicious rituals,' the real criminals were probably already gone."

The couple's defense team successfully argued that search warrants for their home were improperly executed. The Winters left Salem immediately after their release. Their walking tour business was found to have been operated under falsified permits.

"This case bears striking similarities to other gallery thefts in towns with strong metaphysical communities," said FBI Special Agent Diana Chen. "We're continuing to investigate possible connections."

ST. AUGUSTINE RECORD
Spanish Colonial Art Theft Case Collapses
By Matthew Tate, Staff Writer

ST. AUGUSTINE, Fla. (AP) — Local authorities expressed dismay Friday when charges against James and Violet Russell in the theft of Spanish colonial artifacts from the Castillo Art Gallery were dismissed on procedural grounds.

The Russells, who arrived six months ago to open a "paranormal photography" business in the historic district, were accused of orchestrating the disappearance of several 16th-century pieces valued at $900,000. Initial investigations focused on local santeros and psychics after surveillance footage showed ritual candles near the gallery.

"They made us look like superstitious fools," said Elena Vasquez, president of the St. Augustine Spiritual Arts Council. "Our community has been here for generations. The Russells were here for minutes."

The couple departed shortly after their release on bond. Their storefront was found vacant with three months' unpaid rent.

"This case remains under federal investigation," an FBI spokesperson said.

Nineteen

"We need to warn Renee," I said, springing up from the purple velvet armchair. I began to pace. "Like, right now."

"Sit down before you hurt yourself." Liz set her mug down. "We need to think this through."

"Think what through? Jack and Vanessa are married con artists who frame magical communities for art theft. And now they're trying to frame our friend for murder."

"Exactly. Which is why we need to be strategic about this." Liz's long, tie-dye dress swished as she too got to her feet. Both of us were now pacing around The Lounge. "If we bust in like the Kool-Aid Man yelling 'oh yeah!' and telling Renee everything, she might confront Jack. Then they'll know we're onto them."

I slumped back in the chair. "Duck. You're right."

"Of course I'm right. I watch a lot of true crime shows."

"What do we do? Call the FDLE investigator?"

Liz snorted. "Agent Martinez? The one who's already suspicious of Renee and our coven? That'll go well. 'Hi, we have evidence we obtained by breaking into places and using illegal shadow magic. Also, one of us has psychic visions. Please take us seriously. Oh, and we've been snooping around and doing your job.'"

I couldn't help but laugh. When she put it that way, it did sound ridiculous. "We could tell Chris?"

"My boyfriend who specifically stepped down from the case to avoid conflicts of interest? The one who'd have to arrest me if he knew about our B&E adventures?"

"Point taken." I drummed my fingers on the armrest. "But the investigators must have discovered all this already, right? I mean, they're professionals. They have resources we don't."

"Maybe. Or maybe Jack and Vanessa are really good at covering their tracks. Look how many times they've gotten away with this. Obviously they have a heck of a legal team." Liz stopped pacing and stared at the wall of crystals. "You know what this reminds me of?"

"What?"

"Constance Winters. The witch who was wrongly imprisoned in the fifties. The one they're honoring at the solstice festival? She was framed for murder too. The real killers played on people's prejudices against witches to redirect suspicion."

"History repeating itself," I muttered. "But this time we can stop it."

"Exactly." Liz's eyes lit up. "What if we created an anonymous email account and sent everything to the police? The newspaper articles, Thompson's videos—"

"The footage of Jack and Vanessa together!" I sat up straighter. "We could make it look like it came from someone at the gallery."

"Or the bistro."

"Or Pickled."

We grinned at each other, the energy in the room shifting from anxious to conspiratorial.

"I feel like we should be wearing trench coats and sunglasses," I said.

"With fake mustaches."

"Speaking in terrible accents."

We spent the next twenty minutes crafting the perfect anonymous email, debating every word choice. Should we sound official? Casual? Concerned citizen-y? We decided on the basics and proofread the thing one more time.

"Wait," Liz said as we were about to hit send. "What if they trace the IP address?"

I stared at her. It was a computer term I'd heard of, but never really grasped. "The what now?"

"The computer... tracking... thing. I don't know exactly what it is but they always use it on TV shows to catch criminals."

"We shouldn't send it from your shop computer."

"Definitely not. We need to use the library's public computers," she said.

Twenty minutes later, we were power walking through the library's automatic doors, trying to look casual and failing spectacularly. I glanced around, hoping that the elderly librarian who did Crossfit and was seemingly immortal wasn't here to grill us.

Fortunately, she wasn't.

"Stop humming the Mission Impossible theme," I muttered to Liz.

"I can't help it. This is exciting!"

"We're sending an email, not diffusing a bomb."

"Same difference. Now shush and look natural."

We approached the information desk. A kind woman in her twenties with a pin that said "FIGHT BOOK BANS" on her shirt explained how to use the public computers. We nodded and shuffled toward the bank of screens.

We probably looked about as natural as two middle-aged women could while nervously snort-laughing and elbowing each other. But a half hour later, the anonymous email to the cops was sent, the browser history was cleared, and we were back in Liz's shop, feeling simultaneously relieved and terrified.

And praying to the universe that somehow we weren't captured on any camera at the library.

"What now?" I asked.

"We should talk with Renee," Liz said.

"Agreed. I know she wanted to stay out of the case, but she needs to know about Jack."

I reached for my phone and tapped out a text.

> Need to talk, it's urgent

Her response came quickly and I read it aloud.

> Can't right now. Finishing up piano lessons at community center. Meeting Jack at Pickled after for a Wakamole Training Program.

I wrinkled my nose. "What is a Wakamole?"

"It's an advanced pickleball thing." Liz was already reaching for her giant keyring. "She cannot meet that con artist again. We have to get to her before Jack does."

"Community center's what, five minutes away?"

"If we run red lights, three."

"Liz! Your surgery."

She jangled her car keys. "And now I have a perfectly good excuse to drive like a maniac. Let's go."

I kept my eyes mostly shut on the short drive over. Miraculously, Liz was on her best behavior behind the wheel and didn't even use her horn.

The community center was a sprawling one-story building that had seen better days, though someone had tried to brighten it up with murals of local wildlife. We burst through the front doors, startling a chair yoga class.

"Sorry!" I called out as senior citizens in stretchy pants gave us nasty looks. "Which way to the music rooms?"

"Down the hall, past the vending machines," one woman yelled back. "And close the door! We're trying to fire up our chi!"

We found the practice rooms easily enough, mostly because the sound of "Für Elise" played with varying degrees of success led us straight there. Through a window in the door, we could see

Renee sitting at an upright piano next to a pre-teen girl who was concentrating hard on the keys.

"We can't barge in," I whispered.

"Watch me." Liz rapped with her knuckles on the door, then immediately pushed it open without waiting for a response. "Sorry to interrupt, but we have an emergency."

Renee looked up, startled. "What's wrong?"

"Coven business," I said quickly. "It's urgent. We're really sorry about all this."

The girl's eyes lit up. "Are you grandmas really witches? Skibidi!"

I scowled, but said nothing. Grandmas. *Sheesh.* Also, I'd have to ask my daughter what "skibidi" meant later. This was not the moment for Gen Z slang.

"Sarah, why don't we end a few minutes early today?" Renee said smoothly. "You did great with that Bach piece."

Once Sarah had packed up her sheet music and left (but not before asking if we could teach her to cast some "bussin" spells), Renee turned to us with a look of mild panic.

"What's going on? Did something happen with the solstice festival planning?"

"Nope," Liz said, plopping onto a stool. "But you absolutely cannot meet Jack at Pickled today. Or ever again."

"What? Why not?"

I took a deep breath. "Because he's married to Vanessa, and they're both part of an art theft ring that frames metaphysical communities for their crimes."

Renee's face went through several expressions in rapid succession: confusion, disbelief, hurt, and finally, anger. Her hands clenched into fists on the piano keys, creating a discordant clash of notes.

We plowed on, giving her a recap of all that we'd discovered. The newspaper articles, Thompson's security footage, the pattern of art thefts and framed magical communities. With each detail,

Renee's eyes grew wide with disbelief as we showed her the headlines on my phone.

"We also know about the spell you did a week before Dom died. That Amy asked you to cast. I saw it on video at Thompson's." I paused, then added quickly, "But don't worry about that right now. Do you recall anything during your conversations with Jack, now that you know all this about him?"

Renee swiveled back and forth on her stool. "He seemed really interested in local gardening. Which I thought was weird for an investment banker, but..." She trailed off, then suddenly sat up straight. "Oh goddess. I told him about the farm stand at Morning Glory Gardens. About Donna's rare plants."

"That human hemorrhoid," Liz muttered. "He was fishing for information about deadly plants the whole time."

"And I fell for it." Renee's voice cracked. "Like some desperate middle-aged woman so excited about male attention that she spills everything." She slumped forward, resting her forehead on the piano. The keys made a sad, jangled sound. "What am I going to do? He's expecting me at Pickled in twenty minutes for this stupid advanced pickleball training."

"First of all," I said firmly, "you're not desperate or stupid. These people are professional con artists. They've fooled entire towns."

"And art galleries," Liz added. "And police departments."

"Speaking of police..." I exchanged looks with Liz. "We may have anonymously sent everything we found to the FDLE investigator."

Renee lifted her head. "You what?"

"From the library computers!" Liz said quickly. "Very sneaky. Like spies. Well, like middle-aged spies who had to ask the librarian how to convert files to PDFs, but still."

A laugh escaped Renee. "You two are ridiculous." She straightened up, squaring her shoulders. "But thank you. For having my back. For stopping me from walking into whatever trap they're setting."

"That's what friends are for," I said. "Now, about that pickle-ball date..."

"Ghost him," Liz suggested. "Block his number. Tell him you've caught a case of spontaneous combustion."

She snorted and reached for her phone, speaking aloud as she typed. "Emergency with my...coven. Won't... be... at... pickleball. Will take a rain check. Sent!"

We'd all no sooner exhaled when her phone pinged. She lunged for it and read it.

"No worries! How about drinks tonight?"

Renee looked at me. I looked at Liz.

"Say no," Liz said. "Your coven business might go late."

"Tell him it's a female thing and he'll slither back under his rock," I said. "He'll assume it has something to do with periods, or menopause."

"True." She quickly tapped out a text. We all waited in silence for a few beats, but no response came.

"OK," I said. "You're clearly not going for drinks with Jack. But you shouldn't be alone right now. I'm worried for your safety."

"Isn't that overreacting a bit?" Renee asked.

"Nope. These people are dangerous. They've killed once, and who knows what they're planning next," Liz retorted, while digging around in her purse. "You're going to my house. Winston loves playing with Bosco. And before you argue, my house has better security than yours. Chris made me install cameras and motion sensors."

Liz handed Renee a keyring. For some reason, Liz carried multiple sets, all bulging with different keys to unlock who-knows-what.

Renee scowled. "Fine. I'll go home, get Bosco, and head to your place. But that still leaves us with a lot of questions. Like what's Sophia West's connection to all this? Is she involved?"

"Good question." I straightened up. "Wait. What if we—"

"—paid a visit to Sophia at her house?" Liz finished my thought. "She might be able to fill in some blanks for us."

"I was going to suggest inviting her to coffee, but your idea's better. The element of surprise. You've always got your thinking cap on, Liz."

"Well, wait. If we show up unannounced, how do we know whether she'll be home?" Liz asked.

This stumped me for a few seconds. "Oh," I said, reaching for my phone. "I have an idea. Remember that guy I told you about from the solstice charity event?"

"No," Renee said.

"The one who wanted to date you even though he's young enough to be your son?" Liz snickered.

"Luca. His sister works at that fancy Pilates studio. The one with the crystal-infused water that Sophia goes to."

Liz's eyes lit up. "Yes."

I scrolled through my contacts until I found Luca's number. When I'd given him my card at the charity event, he'd texted me immediately. I'd saved his contact info, thinking I might need it someday, and lo and behold, that day was here. The phone barely rang once before he answered.

"Amelia! I was just thinking about you!" His voice was practically vibrating with enthusiasm. "Did you want to get that drink after all?"

"Um, not exactly." I caught Liz making kissy faces at me and turned away. "Actually, I was hoping to talk to your sister. About Pilates."

"Oh." The disappointment in his voice made me feel like I'd kicked a golden retriever puppy.

"Sure, let me text her. She's not in class right now. Want me to find out when she has openings?"

"Actually, I'm not really the Pilates type. I was wondering about Sophia West's schedule. You mentioned she's a regular, right? When will she be at her next class? Do you think your sister knows?"

"For sure! She never misses her classes. Hold on, I'll text my sister."

I put the phone on speaker so Liz could hear. We waited, listening to Luca humming what sounded suspiciously like a Taylor Swift song.

"She texted back!" Luca announced after a minute. "Sophia's got a private lesson at four. She's been super consistent lately — says the crystal-infused water is really helping with her 'life transitions' or something. My sister just talked to her. Sophia said she was at home."

"Perfect," I mouthed to Liz, who was already grabbing her keys.

"So…" Luca's voice took on a hopeful tone. "About that drink…"

"Actually, Luca, I gotta run. Thanks for your help!"

I hung up and looked at my two friends, hoping they were as impressed with my resourcefulness as I was. "We've got two hours before she leaves for Pilates. We could go to her house or ambush her at the studio."

Liz's curls bounced when she shook her head. "I can't wait two hours. Lots to do later. Let's go to her house."

"Fine," I said.

Renee shook her head. "You two are either the bravest or the most foolish sleuths I know."

"Why choose?" Liz grinned. "We excel at both."

Twenty

Sophia West's neighborhood made my usual part of town look like a campground. Not that there was anything wrong with campgrounds — I'd stayed in one when my ex and I had taken our daughter to Yellowstone one year. But this? This was next level wealth.

"Holy crap," I whispered as we drove through streets lined with enormous live oaks creating a canopy over the entrance road to the private development on the outskirts of town. We couldn't even see the homes yet. "I feel like we should've dressed up to drive through here."

Liz snorted. "These folks aren't special. I once delivered bushels of lavender here for a wedding. Worth thousands. The client tipped me twenty bucks and acted like she was being generous. I'm still salty about that."

We approached a guardhouse. A uniformed man stepped out, clipboard in hand.

"Quick," Liz hissed. "What's our story?"

I looked around the Ghost Toaster. There was an apron in the back seat. I reached for it and shoved it at her. "Follow my lead."

Rolling down the window, Liz and I plastered on smiles.

I spoke first. "Hi there! We're here for the West house. Mrs.

West's usual cleaning service had an emergency, so she called our company."

Liz held up the apron.

The guard consulted his clipboard. "I don't see any vendors scheduled..."

"Oh, it was super last minute," I added. "Poor thing was beside herself about her book club meeting tonight. Simply couldn't have company over with dusty baseboards."

I bit my cheek to keep from laughing. Liz's eye twitched. The guard looked uncertain.

"Let me call the house," he said.

"Of course!" Liz chirped.

The guard's hand hesitated over his phone. I swallowed a lump of fear lodged in my throat.

"She's very particular about her cleaning schedule," Liz added. "Bless her heart."

After what felt like an eternity, he waved us through. I waited until we were well past the guardhouse before letting out a slightly hysterical giggle.

"'Bless her heart'?" I wheezed. "Where did that come from?"

"I watch a lot of Real Housewives shows," Liz shot back. "Don't judge. I know you're a 90 Day Fiancé fan."

"True, true," I grumbled.

The West house appeared around a curve, and we both fell silent. The place was massive. It was a sprawling Mediterranean-style mansion with terracotta roof tiles and creamy stucco walls. Perfectly trimmed topiaries lined the circular driveway, and a three-tiered fountain burbled in front of the oversized double doors.

"Yikes," I muttered. "This place probably has its own zip code."

"Look at those huge windows," Liz whispered as we parked. "How do you clean those?"

"I'm sure they pay someone to worry about that."

We climbed out of the car, our sneakers crunching on the

pristine gravel driveway. The front doors were at least twelve feet tall, made of dark wood and fitted with ornate brass hardware. A doorbell panel beside them looked complicated enough to launch a rocket.

I reached for the bell, my mouth parched from nerves.

The chime that echoed through the house sounded like a miniature cathedral organ. Liz and I exchanged wide-eyed looks.

"Maybe she's not—" I started to whisper, but the door swung open.

Sophia West stood there in head-to-toe black Lululemon, looking like she'd stepped out of a fitness influencer's Instagram feed. Her dark hair was swept up in one of those effortlessly messy buns that probably took an hour to style, and she had the glow of a woman who drank a lot of kale juice.

Her perfectly shaped eyebrows shot up. "Yes?"

"Hi," I began. "I'm—"

"The woman from the solstice charity event. The one with the interesting flower crown."

"That's me. Amelia Matthews. And this is my friend Liz."

Sophia's eyes narrowed slightly as she looked between us. "How did you get past security?"

"That's... a funny story, actually." I cleared my throat. "But we need to talk to you about Dominic Harper. And Jack. And your necklace. And some other things."

The color drained from her face so quickly I thought she might faint. She glanced over her shoulder into the house, then back at us. Her eyes narrowed in suspicion.

There was absolutely no way she was going to talk. I gnawed on the inside of my cheek.

"You better come in," she said in an icy tone. "But we don't have much time. Richard could show up at any time. He's playing golf and I don't expect him back, but you never know with him. Come, quickly."

I blinked several times in surprise, both at the fact that she had invited us inside, and by the excessively lavish interior.

We followed Sophia through what felt like a museum of gold and white. Everything gleamed: marble floors, crystal chandeliers, gilt-framed mirrors. As she led us into her cavernous kitchen, I noticed Liz trailing her fingers along the marble countertop in an odd pattern. She was humming something under her breath — barely audible, but it reminded me of a familiar song that I couldn't quite place.

When Sophia turned to face us, Liz quickly dropped her hand, but I caught a whiff of something earthy and sweet, like fresh herbs mixed with morning dew. The scent disappeared so fast I thought I'd imagined it. But something had shifted in Sophia's demeanor. Her shoulders relaxed slightly, and the sharp hostility in her eyes softened to something more vulnerable.

"Kombucha?" Sophia offered, opening a Sub-Zero fridge the size of my entire closet. "It's locally brewed. Infused with crystalline energy."

"Sure," Liz and I chorused.

Sophia fumbled with the bottles, nearly dropping one. She yanked open three different drawers before finding a bottle opener. "I usually have staff for this," she said with a nervous laugh. "I sent my girl out this morning for errands."

I took a sip of the kombucha and immediately regretted it. The "crystalline energy" tasted like someone had steeped gym socks in sparkling water. Liz made a tiny choking sound beside me.

"About Dominic," I said, setting my bottle down carefully on a white marble coaster.

Sophia's perfectly manicured hands trembled as she gripped her own bottle. "I suppose you know about the affair."

"Yes," I said gently. "And about the necklace."

Her free hand went to her throat, as if she was wearing the necklace now. "It's not the real one. It's a replica. The original..." She shuddered and shook her head. "The original belonged to my grandmother. She brought it with her when she fled Europe during World War II. It was one of the few things she managed to save."

"Saved from what?" Liz asked.

"The Nazis. The necklace was part of a collection they'd looted. My grandmother was part of a resistance group that smuggled art and jewelry out of occupied territories." Sophia's voice dropped to barely above a whisper. "Some of the pieces were never returned to their rightful owners. Including the emerald necklace. My family kept it hidden for decades."

"And Dominic found out," I said. It wasn't a question.

She nodded. "I asked him to authenticate it. That's how I met him, I found his authenticating service online. I never intended to sell it. Then we got involved while he was doing that. Romantically. But once he discovered its history..." A single tear rolled down her cheek. "He threatened to expose everything. My grandmother's involvement, the necklace's origin, all of it. Said he'd alert Interpol unless I paid him to keep quiet. I didn't know whether to believe him."

"So you were meeting him in secret to negotiate," I said, thinking of Thompson's security footage.

"Everything got so complicated."

I thought of my vision at the pickleball court, the anger in Dominic's voice. "How so?"

Sophia reached for a tissue from a mother-of-pearl box on the counter. "Oh, he was a charmer. Laid it on thick. After we started sleeping together, he sold the real necklace. Gave me this replica and said no one would know the difference. But that wasn't enough for him." Her voice cracked. "He wanted more money, kept threatening to tell Richard about... everything."

"The affair," Liz said softly.

"God, I was so stupid. He blackmailed me about the necklace and about our relationship." Sophia dabbed at her eyes delicately with her ring finger, careful not to smudge her makeup. "I've never done anything like that before. Seven years of marriage, and I let that snake charm me into throwing it all away. I mean, that and a lot of booze. I met Dom when I was drinking. I'm sober now, I quit after all this happened. But Richard…" Her voice caught. "Richard is a good man. The affair was a horrible mistake. I actually love my husband."

Something about Sophia's vulnerability struck a chord in me. Maybe it was because I'd been through my own messy divorce, or maybe underneath her perfect Instagram-worthy exterior, she was as messy and human as the rest of us. The difference was her mistakes came with much higher stakes than my brief post-divorce Tinder disaster back when I lived in California.

"Then Jack entered the picture. And Dom and Vanessa started dating, which made things even more complicated. I heard Vanessa told people they were engaged but I didn't know."

I squinted, trying to keep everyone and their affairs straight. *Dominic was blackmailing Sophia over a Nazi-looted necklace, carrying on with both Vanessa and Sophia, and somehow Jack was involved too. And now Dom's dead. Got it. When did these people have time to sleep?*

Sophia took a long sip of her drink and continued. "Dom told Jack about my necklace. It was a mess. He told them about the necklace, the affair, all of it."

"How did Dom and Jack know each other?" I piped up.

"Jack and Dom had met through mutual acquaintances. That's what Dom told me. Later I found out that those acquaintances are all criminals." She sighed. "And now Jack is harassing me. He and Vanessa…"

She glanced nervously at the windows, as if expecting someone to be listening. "They're connected to some dangerous people. Art dealers, but not the legal kind. They said if I didn't give them money, or more of my grandmother's jewelry, they'd tell Richard everything."

"So they're blackmailing you, too?" Liz asked.

Sophia's hands were shaking so badly she had to set down her kombucha. "Please, you can't go to the police. If Richard finds out about the affair and the organizations Jack and Vanessa work with, we're toast. I'll ruin my marriage and everything Richard has worked for."

"But a man was murdered," I said gently. "Even though Dom was a snake, justice needs to be served. We can't let Jack get away with this."

"I know." Her voice was barely a whisper. "But I'm terrified I'll be next." The fear in her eyes was too raw to be fake.

I opened my mouth to ask another question but froze at the sound of a man's voice booming through the house.

"Honey! You'll never believe who I ran into at the club!"

Sophia's face went ghost-white. "Richard," she whispered. "He's home."

My heart surged into my throat as footsteps echoed through the cavernous house. Liz and I jumped up from our seats, nearly knocking over our gross kombucha.

"This way," Sophia whispered urgently, gesturing for us to follow her. "Quick!"

We hustled through what felt like an HGTV maze, power-walking through a butler's pantry, a mudroom bigger than my inn's lobby, some kind of gift-wrapping room (seriously?), and finally down into what looked like a climate-controlled wine cellar.

"There's a door that leads to the backyard," Sophia explained in a rushed whisper. "Go through there and cut across the tennis court. The service gate is unlocked."

"Sophia?" Richard's voice sounded closer. "Are you in the kitchen? Is that the maid's car? It's so ugly, I hate it parked out front of the house."

"Coming, darling!" she called back, her voice impressively steady. To us, she whispered, "Please. Don't tell anyone what I told you. I'll figure something out, I promise."

As we slipped through the wine cellar door, I caught a glimpse of Sophia straightening her shoulders and plastering on a bright smile, like an actress preparing to go onstage. The heavy door clicked shut behind us, and Liz and I were alone among dozens of bottles of outrageously expensive wine.

"Yikes," I muttered, trying to get my bearings in the dim lighting.

"Tell me about it." Liz grabbed my arm and pointed. "There's the door."

I followed her outside. "Yeah, we can't be caught when he comes down here to pick out a bottle of 1986 Château Whatever for dinner."

As we speed-walked across the meticulously manicured grounds, trying to look like we belonged there, I couldn't erase the image of Sophia's face when she talked about the dangerous people tied to Jack and Vanessa.

"Well, that was useful," Liz said as we finally reached the Ghost Toaster. We climbed in and roared off. Well, maybe not roared. More like chugged steadily. Out the side mirror, I could see Richard standing in the middle of the driveway, hands on hips.

"I wonder why Sophia was so chatty?" I asked as we zipped down the road. "I was pretty sure she wasn't going to talk with us when she opened the door."

"Let's say I gave her a little encouragement," Liz said with a mysterious smile. "A simple trust charm. Nothing manipulative. Just helped her feel safe enough to share what she already wanted to tell us."

"Wow. Your magic is really coming along. I'm proud of you."

"But that Richard guy. I don't like him at all." She caressed the steering wheel. "How could he call the Ghost Toaster ugly?"

The next morning, I found Jimbo in the inn's dining room, arranging succulent cuttings in tiny terracotta pots. My guests had enjoyed the previous day's seminar so much that they all asked for a follow-up class.

They were gathered around him like eager kindergarteners at story time, hanging on his every word about proper propagation techniques.

"And that's why you gotta let the ends callus over before you stick 'em in dirt," he drawled, holding up what looked like a tree branch, but was probably some rare plant specimen. "Otherwise, you'll get root rot faster than a gator can snap up a hot dog."

The honeymooners from Wisconsin exchanged bewildered glances while the psychic retreat ladies furiously scribbled notes. I couldn't tell if they were more fascinated by plant care or Jimbo's endless supply of Florida-themed metaphors.

I cleared my throat. "Hey, Jimbo? Got a minute?"

He looked up, his face brightening. "Sure thing, Miss Amelia. I was showing our guests here how to grow their own garden friends."

I'd given Jimbo a substantial raise last month, partly because he deserved it and partly because I felt guilty about how often I dumped inn duties on him while investigating murders. The fact that he seemed to genuinely enjoy being the default innkeeper only made me feel marginally better about it.

"I need to run an errand," I said, trying to sound casual. "Would you mind—"

"Holding down the fort?" He grinned. "No problem. Me and these fine folks are about to start a discussion on communicating with spider plants. Did you know they're excellent listeners?"

The psychic retreat ladies nodded sagely. The honeymoon couple looked like they were questioning their choice of vacation destination.

I left Jimbo explaining the spiritual benefits of talking to houseplants and headed for my car. Liz had wanted to come with me to Morning Glory Gardens, but today was Wellness Wednesday, when folks over the age of sixty-five got a ten percent discount on all crystals. She'd described the once-weekly sale as "mayhem," so she had to stay there all day.

The drive out to Donna's greenhouse felt longer alone. Every shadow in the scrubby landscape looked menacing, and I kept thinking of that grabby burgundy fern. I pulled into the gravel lot, noticing fewer cars than last time. No farm stand today, only the looming Victorian greenhouse with its clouded glass panels and creeping vines.

I walked toward the greenhouse. Donna Anderson emerged from a side door, looking exactly as intimidating as I remembered in her cargo pants and UV protection shirt. Her steel-gray hair was still pulled into that severe bun, but today she wore thick gardening gloves that reached her elbows.

Her eyes narrowed when she saw me. "You've got some nerve showing up here."

"I can explain—" I started, but she cut me off.

"Breaking into my greenhouse wasn't enough? Now you're back for what? More corporate espionage? Another attempt to steal my rare specimens?"

I scowled. "Corporate espionage? No. I'm an innkeeper who is trying to clear her coven leader's name on a murder charge."

She wrinkled her nose, as if something smelled bad. "What?"

"Dominic Harper?" I looked at her expectantly.

"Who?"

"The gallery owner. Murdered on the pickleball court four days ago. Poisoned. By rare oleander." I folded my arms accusatorially. While I hadn't anticipated being confrontational with Donna, my patience was reaching its limit with everyone and everything.

She seemed as though she had no idea what I was talking about.

For a beat she paused while she sized me up. Finally, she spoke. "Come inside."

She led me through a different door than last time, into what appeared to be another section of the greenhouse. The plants in this part, I recognized. Still, I kept my arms tucked close to my sides, not trusting any of the foliage. After our last visit, I wouldn't have been surprised if even the ordinary-looking ferns had developed a taste for human flesh.

"These are all safe," Donna said, as if reading my mind. "Medicinal herbs, mostly. Chamomile, echinacea, ordinary stuff you'd find in any tea shop." She gestured to rows of lush plants with familiar-looking leaves. "Nothing in here will try to consume you. Or poison you."

"That's reassuring." I couldn't help noticing she'd specified that nothing in *this* section would try to eat me.

The air here was different from the other part of the greenhouse, lighter somehow, fragrant with mint and lavender instead of that sickly-sweet decay smell I remembered. Sunlight filtered through the glass panels, creating dappled patterns on the slate floor. It was almost peaceful, if you ignored the ominous rustling coming from behind the locked door at the far end of the room. I hoped it was her son, but then again, anything was possible in here.

Donna moved to a weathered potting bench and began methodically cleaning up scattered soil and dead leaves. "So," she said, not looking up from her task, "you think I supplied the poison that killed this Dominic Harper fellow." It wasn't a question.

"The evidence points to a rare variety of oleander. One that only grows in Central Florida." I watched her hands as she worked, noting how precisely she handled each tool despite the thick gloves. "And you have quite the collection of rare, potentially lethal plants."

She snorted. "I also have rare, potentially lethal knowledge. Doesn't mean I go around using it to murder people." She straightened up and fixed me with a penetrating stare. "Start from the beginning. Tell me everything. And this time, try not to act like a bad spy novel character. Please be concise. I don't have all the time in the world for malarkey."

I gave her a quick recap of Dominic's death and how I was in a coven and trying to clear Renee's name. Her face didn't register any emotion or show surprise when I started talking about witches. When I was done, an uncomfortable silence lingered while a bead of sweat ran down my back, into the waistband of my capri pants.

Seconds ticked by and she didn't say a word. Finally, I couldn't stand it.

"Surely, you've heard the news about Dominic. It's all over town. All over the TV news and the papers."

"I don't consume news. Not at this time of year." Her mouth slanted.

I screwed up my face. "W-why?"

"Because it's the anniversary of my mother's death. You might have heard of her. Constance Winters?" She aggressively dug into a pot, pulling out dirt and wiggling earthworms.

"Constance Winters?" I repeated, my voice barely a whisper. "The witch who was wrongly imprisoned? The one they're honoring at the solstice festival?"

Donna's hands stilled over the pot of wriggling earthworms. "The one who died in prison before she could see her name cleared. Yes. The one who wasted away in prison and refused my visits because she didn't want me to see her in that state." Her voice had an edge sharper than her pruning shears. "Yes. My mother."

I gripped the edge of the potting bench, my knees suddenly weak. The summer solstice festival, the pardoning ceremony — it all took on a different meaning now.

"I was eight when they arrested her," Donna continued, her fingers mechanically separating soil clumps. "Sent to live with my grandmother in Tennessee. A woman who thought magic was the devil's work, and tried to beat it out of me." She gave a harsh laugh. "Didn't take. I should've run far from Florida, but I came home, bought this property, and worked my own magic by myself."

"I'm so sorry," I managed, though the words felt pathetically inadequate.

"Every June, like clockwork, the papers drag it all up again. 'Remember the Winters Case?' 'Justice Denied.' And now?" She gestured sharply with a trowel. "Now that those high school students proved what we knew all along — that she was innocent — it's everywhere. TV specials, newspaper retrospectives, true crime podcasts. Everyone wanting to talk about how the system failed her. How tragic it all was. I hate every second of it."

A delicate-looking vine near my elbow trembled, responding to Donna's agitation. I edged away.

"Understandable. But they're pardoning her at the festival," I said softly. "To honor her memory."

"Honor?" Donna's laugh was bitter as wormwood. "Where was that honor decades ago? Where was it when my mother was dying alone in a prison cell? When my grandmother was forcing me to attend etiquette classes instead of teaching me the family's plant knowledge?" She yanked off one glove and slapped it on the bench. "So no, I don't read the news. Not in June. I stay here with my plants. They, at least, don't pretend to care only when it's convenient."

I stood there, struck dumb by the weight of history crushing into the present. All my questions about oleander and poison suddenly seemed small and intrusive. Nervous, I licked my lips.

She spoke before I could. "But you didn't come here to hear my story, and now I'm quite interested in yours. If you and your sidekick had told me what you were looking for the other day, I'd have helped you."

I cringed. "Sorry. Sometimes my friend gets a little carried away. She's in community theater."

Donna gave me a hard stare, one that told me she wasn't going to put up with any further shenanigans.

"Tell me more about this Jack person's wife," Donna said, turning back to her potting bench. "What does she look like?"

"Vanessa? Young, beautiful in that Instagram influencer way. Dark hair, perfect makeup and non-frizzy hair, even in Florida humidity, which should be impossible." I paused, thinking. "Always dressed like she's about to do a photo shoot for a luxury brand catalog."

I pulled up one of the videos sent by Thompson and pressed play. Donna cupped her hands around the screen.

"Is she in her thirties? Maybe twenties? I can't tell ages anymore." She stripped off her other glove. "Tall? Better dressed than most people in these parts?"

I wondered if that was an indictment on my casual outfit but immediately dismissed the thought. My stomach did a little flip. "Yes! You've seen her?"

"Oh yes. She came here about a month ago, claimed she was a journalist doing a story on traditional plant medicine and indigenous Florida herbs." Donna's mouth twisted. "Said she was writing for some lifestyle magazine. Asked a lot of questions about my specimens."

"Let me guess. The toxic ones?"

"Precisely. I didn't tell her anything." Donna moved to a sink and began washing her hands with methodical precision. "Then two nights later, my security cameras caught someone who looked remarkably like the alleged journalist helping herself to clippings from my oleander collection. After hours."

I swallowed hard. "Did you call the police?"

Donna's laugh was as dry as dead leaves. "I have my own security system." She whistled sharply, and a massive dark shape emerged from behind a row of potted trees. "Meet Rocky."

I froze as what appeared to be a small, charcoal-colored horse padded toward us. It took my brain several seconds to process that it was, in fact, a dog. One that looked like it could eat my Freddie in one bite and still have room for dessert. Heck, it looked like it could eat *me* in two bites.

"What...what is it?" I asked.

"A dog," Donna said, clearly exasperated.

"I mean, what kind? He's large." He had to weigh as much as I did.

"Cane Corso. Rocky convinced that woman to leave," Donna said with grim satisfaction. "Though not before she'd harvested a few clippings of what she came for."

I tried not to picture what "convinced her to leave" might have entailed. If Donna's plants were nightmare fuel, her guard dog was something straight out of a horror movie.

"Why didn't you report the break-in?" I asked, keeping one eye on Rocky, who had settled at Donna's feet like an extremely muscular shadow. He sighed contentedly. Probably he was a good boy, but I wasn't going out of my way to give him a belly rub.

She fixed me with a look that could have withered her entire poison collection. "The last time I trusted law enforcement, my mother died in prison." Rocky sat up. She scratched him behind his ears, his massive head at her waist. "I prefer to handle things my way now."

"Reasonable." I warily eyed Rocky.

"There is one thing," Donna said. "That particular strain of oleander? It leaves a distinctive chemical signature. Any decent lab could trace it back to my greenhouse." She pulled out a thick ledger. "Which is why I keep meticulous records of everyone who visits."

She hesitated, then fixed me with a penetrating stare. "My mother died because evidence that could have cleared her name was ignored. Now these people are trying to frame another witch." Her jaw tightened. "I won't let that happen again."

"I'd like to give you something. If I leave you alone here, do you promise not to touch anything?" Donna asked.

"I promise. Not even a leaf."

"Good. But I'll let Rocky keep watch." She made some sort of hand signal and bizarrely, he seemed to be paying attention.

For five long, sweaty minutes, I stood there, sneaking glances at the dog. He fixated on me, which was unsettling. Finally, Donna returned carrying a folder. She handed it to me.

"I may not trust law enforcement, but I trust witches to protect their own. Use this however you need to."

I flipped through the papers. "Whoa," I whispered. "Thank you."

"My instinct tells me I should trust you. My brain says I shouldn't." She heaved a sigh. "Now, go."

I thanked her again, then hurried to my car. Behind me, Rocky's deep bark echoed through the greenhouse, and I swore I heard Donna say, "Good boy. Keep watch."

My phone buzzed. Oliver. We had plans for the night, and he was texting to see what time he should come over for dinner.

I smiled, already thinking about the information I held in my hand, and how good it would feel to decompress with him after all this.

Twenty-Two

After the events of the week, all I wanted was comfort food and quiet time. I managed both, whipping up a late pasta dinner in my apartment kitchen while Oliver sat at my small table, reviewing my hastily scrawled notes about our conversation with Sophia. The scent of garlic and herbs filled the air, mingling with the vanilla-scented candle I'd lit earlier.

Freddie lounged on the windowsill, his orange bulk taking up the entire space. Every few minutes, he'd crack open one eye to make sure we weren't eating without him, then go back to his important business of pretending to nap.

"Sophia confirmed it. Huh," Oliver said, shifting my notebook pages. "Jack and Vanessa are using their art theft playbook here in Cypress Grove, like they did in those other metaphysical communities."

I stirred the sauce, adding a pinch more basil. "Yeah, but this time they've escalated to murder. And now they're blackmailing Sophia with the affair and her antique necklace. And Dom was carrying on with both Sophia and Vanessa. It's so messy. Dom charmed Sophia into an affair, blackmailed her over the necklace, then told Jack and Vanessa, who started squeezing her for more. It's like a horrible soap opera. Only real."

"The necklace situation explains some things," Oliver mused. "Though I think there's more to it than even Sophia's telling us."

"Probably." I tasted the sauce. Perfect. "The way she talked about those 'dangerous people' Jack and Vanessa work with..." I shook my head.

Oliver looked up from the notes, his expression serious. "You're worried about her."

"I am." I started plating the pasta. "But I'm more worried about what they might do to Renee. Or us, for that matter. If they find out that Liz and I know all this stuff, I'm worried."

I let out a long sigh.

"I'm worried about that as well, hon." Oliver's gaze met mine.

Freddie chose that moment to abandon his windowsill post, sauntering over to weave between my legs. "No way, mister," I told him. "You already had dinner. And treats. And more treats when you gave me those sad eyes."

"He's got you wrapped around his paw," Oliver chuckled.

"Like you're any better? I saw you sneaking him tuna last week."

We settled in to eat, the comfortable silence broken only by the distant sound of my guests returning from their evening activities. Someone upstairs was playing meditation music—probably the Wisconsin newlyweds, who'd gotten really into crystal healing since arriving.

"About earlier," Oliver said suddenly, setting down his fork. "On the phone. When I said—"

"I love you too," I blurted, then felt my face flush. Smooth, Amelia. Real smooth.

But Oliver's grin was worth my awkwardness. "Yeah?"

"Yeah." I reached across the table and squeezed his hand. "I've been wanting to say it for a while. I was just. You know."

"Scared?"

"Cautious," I corrected, though he wasn't wrong. "After the divorce, I wasn't sure I'd ever want to say those words again. But you make it easy."

His thumb traced circles on my palm, sending little shivers up my arm. "You make it easy too."

Freddie chose that moment to jump onto the table, nearly knocking over my wine glass. "Hey!" I scolded, but he gave me his most innocent look before settling between us like a furry orange chaperone.

"Speaking of scary things," I said, scratching behind Freddie's ears, "I need to figure out how to tell Jenny about... all of this." I gestured vaguely at everything — the inn, my psychometry, the whole witch situation.

And Oliver. I need to tell my daughter about him.

"Ah." Oliver sat back, considering. "The 'hey honey, your mom's a witch now' conversation."

"Yes, that, too. Like, 'Remember how I used to bake cookies? Well, now I solve murders with my psychic powers and hang out with shadow-melding waitresses.' She's going to think I've lost it."

"Kids are more adaptable than we think. Look how she handled the divorce."

I nodded, remembering how Jenny had been my rock through that whole mess. "True. But this is different. This is supernatural."

"And she's Gen Z. They're pretty open to that stuff, right?"

"I guess." I pushed my plate away, suddenly not very hungry. "I don't want her to worry. Or think I'm having some kind of midlife crisis."

"Aren't you?" Oliver's eyes twinkled. "I mean, you did move across the country, inherit a haunted inn, join a coven, and start solving murders."

"When you put it that way, it sounds absolutely bananas."

"It sounds brave," he corrected. "And Jenny will see that too." He paused, his expression softening. "You know, from everything you've told me about her, she seems like someone who'd understand taking a leap of faith. Following your heart."

My throat tightened. Jenny had always been the brave one, heading off to college in another state without a backward glance while shrugging off her parents' nasty divorce. She was such a resilient kid. "I hope so. I can't wait for you to meet her next month."

"Me too." He smiled. "Though I have to admit, I'm a little nervous. What if she thinks I'm some nerdy professor who's way too into paranormal Florida history?"

"She'll love you," I said, meaning it. "Because I do."

The words hung in the air between us, simple and true. Oliver reached across the table and took my hand. "Come on. Let's find something mindless on TV and just... be."

We migrated to my small sofa, some home renovation show playing quietly in the background. Oliver's arm was warm around my shoulders, and Freddie had claimed his usual spot on the back of the couch, occasionally batting at Oliver's hair. In that moment, surrounded by two of the beings I trusted most, I felt completely at peace. I let go of all thoughts about Jack's murder and Renee's predicament and succumbed to Oliver's calm vibe.

I must have dozed off at some point because when I opened my eyes, he was sound asleep, his head tipped back, and glasses slightly askew. The TV had moved on to some infomercial about miracle cleaning products. I carefully removed his glasses, setting them on the side table, and pulled the throw blanket over him. He looked so peaceful, I couldn't bring myself to wake him.

My phone buzzed in my pocket. Whoa. It was a message from Thompson.

Security footage from the gallery. Jack and Vanessa are there + hauling out everything that's not nailed down. Sending clip now.

I pulled up the grainy video. Two figures moved through the shadows of the gallery. Even in the poor lighting, I could make out Jack's silver hair. And Vanessa's long ponytail.

I glanced at Oliver, still sleeping soundly. For a split second, I considered waking him. But, no. He had an early class tomorrow, and frankly, I didn't want to put him in danger. Whatever was happening at the gallery, it wasn't his business. This was a coven issue, and unlike other covens around town, the Sisters of Hecate were all women.

Women who looked out for each other and who didn't depend on men to rescue them. We'd learned that few people in this world wanted anything to do with middle-aged women. We had to save ourselves.

I scribbled a quick note: *Had to check something out. Don't worry. Will explain everything later. xo — A*

Then I texted Liz.

> SOS. Meet me at the gallery. It might be worth telling Chris that Jack and Vanessa are moving lots of stuff out of the gallery. FDLE seems MIA.

Her response was immediate:

> OMG. On my way. Will call Chris from car.

I crept into my bedroom and changed into black yoga pants and a dark long-sleeved shirt. My hands shook slightly as I tied my hair back. This felt different than our previous amateur sleuthing adventures. More dangerous. More final.

Freddie watched from the doorway as I laced up my sneakers, his blue eyes gleaming in the dim light. "Keep an eye on Oliver for me, okay?" I whispered, stroking his head.

He responded with an eye squint, which made me think he'd possibly understood me. Or he was thinking about a second dinner.

With one last look at the slumbering Oliver on the couch, I slipped out of the apartment and into the sticky Florida night.

When I cruised by the gallery building, the Ghost Toaster was already in the back lot, looking particularly ethereal in the glow of a lone streetlamp. Liz probably shouldn't have parked there. It was too obvious of a place if we were going to watch the gallery.

I circled the block and pulled the car into a space on a nearby street, then walked to the back lot. There, I found Liz crouched behind a dumpster, which seemed both completely ridiculous and totally on-brand for us at this point.

"Over here," she whispered loudly. "And watch out for the—"

My foot squished in something. "—puddle," she finished.

"Please tell me that's water from the AC unit," I muttered, tiptoeing toward her hiding spot.

"Definitely water. Probably." She wrinkled her nose. "I told Chris. Well, I texted him. I didn't want a lecture."

"Good. Although I have to admit, hiding behind a dumpster isn't exactly how I pictured spending my Wednesday night. I should be in my PJs watching the Tonight Show."

A shadow detached itself from the wall, making both of us jump. "Ladies," Amy's voice floated toward us. "Y'all really need to work on your stealth game."

She materialized fully, still wearing her bistro uniform. Unlike us, she actually looked graceful lurking in dark alleys. The shadows around her seemed to pulse and throb.

"I was closing up when I saw them go in," she whispered. "They're in Dominic's old office. Only me and Marcus working tonight, and he's already left. I'd stay to help but I've got to finish the deposit and set the alarm. The side door's unlocked if you want a closer look."

After Amy dissolved back into the darkness, Liz and I exchanged looks.

"I'll be honest, I'm not sure why we're here. I acted on total impulse when I got Thompson's text," I said. "I guess we could take photos? Or observe? Maybe this wasn't the best plan."

"We could get closer; take a quick peek." She glanced at the door. "Just to make sure we know where they are when the police arrive."

"If the police arrive. There's no guarantee."

"Chris will probably come roaring up at any minute. Let's just keep an eye out for Jack and Vanessa."

Through the windows of the bistro, I could see Amy counting out the register, alone in the empty restaurant. The Sunday night crowd had cleared out hours ago. The street was deserted — everyone was either home watching TV or at the bars closer to downtown.

Liz moved away from the dumpster, toward the building.

I knew it was a bad idea, but I followed her anyway. We slipped through the side door into the building's dark hallway.

"I can't hear anything from here," Liz whispered. We pressed ourselves against the cool brick wall, trying to blend into the shadows. "But these old brick buildings usually have ventilation grates. There might be one upstairs where we can listen in. I think the stairs are down there. I used to know someone who rented a ceramic studio up there."

She pointed to the end of the hallway.

"Are you suggesting we crawl around looking for air vents like we're in a spy movie?"

"Got any better ideas?"

Going home, snuggling next to Oliver, and sleeping? But no, this was my idea. We were here and the only way through this was through. We had to help Renee.

"Well, no," I mumbled.

The longer we stood there doing nothing, the more anxious I felt about whatever was happening in Dom's office. We crept toward the stairs, the carpet runner doing little to muffle our steps.

We'd almost reached an old water fountain in the corner of the hallway when voices drifted through the door to the gallery.

"...has to be tonight," Vanessa was saying, her voice sharp with anger. "We're running out of time."

"The FDLE has been in town all week," Jack replied. "If we don't—"

A floorboard creaked beneath my foot, the sound like a scream in the quiet hallway.

The voices stopped.

Liz and I froze, hardly daring to breathe. For a moment, complete silence filled the hall.

Then footsteps approached, the door flung open, and a familiar face poked out.

"Well." Jack looked amused. "Looks like we have company."

Vanessa joined him in the doorway. Liz and I were basically cornered at the end of the hall. Our options were to run upstairs, or get caught.

"How convenient," Vanessa added, her tone dripping with false sweetness. "I was wondering if we'd see the dynamic duo before we left town."

Twenty-Three

"Before you do anything stupid," I said, my voice shaking despite my best efforts to sound brave, "you should know the police are on their way."

Jack's smile faltered slightly as he glanced at Vanessa. "This complicates things."

"Bull," Vanessa said. "They're faking it."

"We're not," Liz retorted in a shrill tone that indicated that we might indeed be lying. "I'm dating the police chief."

"I'm dating the police chief," Vanessa mocked.

My palms were sweaty, and my heart was thumping so hard I felt dizzy. We were trapped in a dark hallway with two people who'd already killed once. If I screamed, would Amy even hear me? Or would that mean I'd get shot on the spot?

"We can't let them walk out of here," Vanessa hissed. "They know too much."

"About what?" Liz asked, her voice surprisingly calm. Almost conversational. How was she so collected? I felt like I might throw up or pass out or both. I wrapped my hand around Liz's wrist and tried to subtly tug her toward the door to the stairwell.

"Don't play dumb," Vanessa snapped. "You've been following us. Poking around. Asking questions."

"We could leave," Jack said quietly. "We have what we came for."

Vanessa pulled something from her pocket — a small glass vial filled with clear liquid. Crapola. I knew without asking what was in that bottle. The same thing that had killed Dominic.

"No." Vanessa's voice was cold. "They'll talk."

"That wasn't part of the plan," Jack protested. "We agreed, no more—"

"Plans change," Vanessa cut him off, her eyes glittering with something that made my skin crawl. "Like they did before."

Jack sighed, and the sound was worse than any threat. It sounded like resignation. He reached under his golf jacket and pulled out a small handgun. The sight of it made my stomach plummet to my feet. This was really happening. And I wasn't prepared. Not that one prepared for scenarios like this.

I sent a silent prayer to the universe, to Chris, to Thompson. Someone, something, had to step in and save us.

"Inside," he said quietly, gesturing toward the gallery entrance with the gun. "Both of you."

We had no choice. I went first, Liz behind me, our feet scuffing against the polished concrete floor. A few strategic spotlights cast pools of light on the remaining paintings. Most of the recent exhibition had already been packed away, leaving the gallery feeling eerily empty. The space felt cavernous without the usual crowd of wine-sipping art patrons.

"Over there," Jack directed, pointing toward the back wall with the gun. "By the Rothko knockoff."

I almost wanted to laugh at that. But the cold metal gun barrel pointed at us killed any hint of irony.

"Against the wall," Vanessa snapped, pointing to a spot between two huge abstract paintings. "Both of you."

We marched over. I couldn't help noticing that the paintings didn't have price tags. Even facing possible death, my brain fixated on random details. Maybe that was a coping mechanism; focus on the small stuff so you didn't have to process the big, terrifying reality that catastrophic things are happening around you.

"What are we going to do?" I muttered to Liz.

"Shut up," Vanessa hissed, digging through a cardboard box near Dominic's old desk. "Where are those ropes? Jack, did you move them?"

"They were right there," he said, keeping the gun trained on us. His silver hair gleamed under the gallery spotlights. "In the box with all the extension cords and chargers."

"Well, they're not here now." Vanessa upended the box, spilling a tangled mass of black cords onto the floor.

"Looking for something to tie us up with?" I asked, unable to help myself, babbling nervously. "You know how it is with cords. You have approximately eight million of them but can never find the one you need. Like phone chargers. They multiply like rabbits until you actually want one."

"I said *shut up*." Vanessa's face was flushed with anger as she kicked through the pile. I watched her slip the vial into her pocket.

"There's probably a whole drawer of them somewhere," I continued, my mouth apparently disconnected from my survival instinct. Or maybe I was trying to come to some common ground with them. Wasn't that what you were supposed to do if taken hostage? Had I read that somewhere? "Tangled up with old Christmas lights and those weird cables that nobody knows what they're for but you're afraid to throw away."

"Amelia," Liz whispered urgently. "Maybe now isn't the time for commentary on universal cord struggles?"

Vanessa whirled around. "One more word about cords and I'll... wait. Found some. Zip ties. Better than cords anyway."

My heart sank. Zip ties were definitely worse than random tangled cords. I'd watched enough true crime shows to know they only got tighter if you struggled.

"Finally," Jack muttered. "Something's going right tonight."

As Vanessa approached with the zip ties, I caught Liz moving her fingers in tiny patterns at her side. She was muttering something, so quiet I could barely hear. A spell? I desperately hoped it was a spell, preferably something that would turn Jack and Vanessa into toads. Or at least make them really, really clumsy.

"Hands behind your backs," Jack ordered, but his voice had a weary quality to it, like he was already tired of playing the villain. "Look, this isn't personal. You got in the way."

"Not personal?" I couldn't help but snort. "You literally pretended to be interested in my friend so you could set her up on murder charges. That feels pretty personal to me."

"The coven was an unexpected complication," Vanessa said, stopping a few feet from us. She appraised us, as if she was critiquing our outfits. "We usually don't have to deal with actual witches. Most of these metaphysical tourist towns are full of frauds."

"Lucky us," Liz said, still moving her fingers. "We're authentic."

The temperature in the room seemed to drop suddenly, and I wasn't sure if it was fear, or something Liz was cooking up with her incantations. Either way, I kept talking, hoping to buy us some time.

"So what's the plan here?" I asked, trying to keep my voice steady. "Tie us up and then what? Because I have guests at the inn who'll notice if I don't show up for breakfast. And let me tell you, the Wisconsin couple gets really cranky without their morning coffee. Plus my cat. He'll notice."

A wave of nausea washed over me. Oliver. Freddie. *My daughter Jenny.*

I couldn't die now. Not when I hadn't fully explored my relationship with Oliver. Not when I'd finally embraced my powers. Not when I hadn't told my daughter about witchcraft, about what was possible for women in midlife and beyond.

"Speaking of plans," Liz said, her voice taking on an edge I'd never heard, "why don't you let us in on how you really killed Dominic? Before you try to pin it on our friend Renee?"

Vanessa's lip curled. "Your precious coven leader? Please. She made it so easy. All those late-night rituals, sneaking around. Cops already think she's guilty. I'll bet we can even pin your deaths on her."

"Because you set her up!" The fury in Liz's voice made even Jack flinch. "You preyed on a woman who's been nothing but kind to everyone in this town. Who teaches piano to kids and delivers food to the elderly and transports blood as a side hustle, for heaven's sake."

She was right. The more I thought about it, the angrier I got. Renee, who worked three jobs and still found time to help every member of our coven. Who'd welcomed me with open arms when I first moved here. Who baked cookies for the homeless shelter and fostered senior dogs and never, ever said no to someone in need.

"You picked her because she was vulnerable," I said, my own anger building. "Because she was lonely and single. You probably thought middle-aged women were easy targets, right? That we're so desperate for attention we'd never suspect anything?"

"That's usually how it works," Vanessa said with a shrug that made me want to dunk her perfect manicure in acid. "Lonely women are so grateful for male attention they don't ask questions. Although I have to admit, Jack was amazing with the silver fox pickleball champion act."

"It wasn't an act. I love pickleball," Jack said peevishly, but Vanessa shot him a look that could have peeled paint.

"The oleander in Dominic's water bottle," Liz pressed. "When did you put it there? And which one of you did? And why?"

"A lot of questions for a woman who's about to die," Jack groused.

"During the game. I did," Vanessa said. Jack kept the gun trained on us, his arm steady despite his obvious discomfort.

I could smell Vanessa's expensive perfume — something floral and cloying — as she stepped closer. "Not that it matters now, but I slipped into the locker room while everyone was focused on your pathetic excuse for a pickleball match. Dom always carried two bottles with him. With his stupid electrolytes. So predictable. Renee going into the bathroom when you all had your little pickleball spat made it that much easier to blame the entire thing on her."

My eyes flickered away from her face. In a flash, I saw her nails. Wine red.

"The paddle in the bathroom," I blurted, the memory clicking into place. "That was yours. The perfect manicure, the red nails. You were spying on Jack and Dom that day, weren't you? Listening to them argue about the forgeries."

Vanessa's smirk faltered slightly. "You have no idea how annoying it was, playing dumb. Having to pretend I didn't know about the business and worst of all, pretending to be his girlfriend." She flexed her fingers, her nails like bloody talons. "I had to make sure Dom wasn't going to expose us. When I heard him threatening Jack that day at Pickled, I knew we had to act fast. I carried the oleander with me at all times, just in case."

Sweat trickled down my back, making my shirt cling uncomfortably. The gallery's air conditioning hummed overhead, but it didn't seem to be doing much against the Florida night air seeping in through the old windows. Or maybe that was the fear taking over.

"You set up Renee and didn't care where Dom died, even if it was in public," I said, my voice barely a whisper. "You needed him dead before he could expose your forgery ring."

"Well, that and the fact that he was a little too clingy with me. God, he was so annoying. But our plan worked perfectly," Vanessa preened, her heels clicking on the polished concrete as she paced in front of us. "Public place, witnesses, medical emergency. Plus, we got to frame your little coven in the process. Two birds, one stone."

Something in me snapped. Maybe it was her smug tone, or the casual way she talked about murder, or the sheer audacity of people who thought they could waltz into our town and prey on women like us.

"You know what your mistake was?" I felt the anger rising in my chest, hot and fierce. The spotlights cast harsh shadows across Vanessa's face, making her look more ghoulish than glamorous. "You thought we were sitting ducks. Poor, sad, middle-aged women. But here's the thing about women our age: we've seen it all. We've survived divorce, death, disappointment. We've raised kids and buried parents and reinvented ourselves a dozen times over."

"Who cares," Vanessa snapped, but I was on a roll.

"And you know what else?" I continued, noticing that Liz's finger movements had become more deliberate. The temperature in the room seemed to drop another few degrees. "We're done being underestimated by people like you."

I glanced at the gun in Jack's hand, calculating distances. Maybe if I moved fast enough... but no, that was stupid. This wasn't an action movie, and I wasn't exactly Jackie Chan.

That's when the brick wall behind Jack and Vanessa rippled like water, and Amy stepped through it as casually as if she was walking through a beaded curtain. Her bistro apron was still on.

I let out an undignified yelp of surprise. Even though I'd seen her shadow-melding before, it was still shocking. Jack spun around, the gun wavering. Vanessa shrieked and stumbled backward.

"Y'all picked the wrong town to commit murder in," Amy drawled, her form flickering slightly in the dim gallery lights. "And the wrong women to mess with."

The shadows around her seemed to pulse and throb, darker than the darkest paint on the fake Rothko behind us. The temperature dropped another ten degrees, and I could see Jack's breath forming little clouds in the suddenly frigid air.

"What... what are you?" Vanessa's voice had lost its smug edge, replaced by something close to panic.

With Jack distracted by Amy's shadowy entrance, I launched

myself at him. My rational brain screamed that this was insane, but my body moved anyway. We collided hard, my shoulder ramming into his chest. The gun clattered to the floor and skittered away under a display pedestal.

Jack recovered right away, grabbing for my arms, but months of hauling suitcases up the inn's stairs had given me more upper body strength than he'd expected. We grappled awkwardly, knocking into a stack of packing crates.

"The door!" Amy shouted as Vanessa made a break for it, her stilettos *tap-tap-tapping* on the concrete floor. But the shadows around Amy surged forward like a wave, wrapping around Vanessa's ankles. She stumbled, pitching forward with a shriek. Somehow, because of the shadows, she was unable to move. It was as if she was hogtied with invisible rope.

Meanwhile, Liz had finished whatever spell she'd been working on. She thrust her hands forward and Jack went flying backward as if hit by an invisible truck. His head cracked against the wall with a sickening thud, and he slumped to the ground.

"Whoa," I cried out, staring at his body. "Did you kill him?"

"Just knocked out," Liz said, though she looked a bit uncertain. "Probably."

Amy walked over and retrieved the gun. I sagged against a wall, trying to catch my breath. "That was... that was..."

"Pretty badass," Liz finished, grinning despite the tension. "Especially your tackle. Where'd you learn that?"

"Hauling guest luggage," I panted. "You'd be amazed how many people pack like they're never coming home."

Twenty-Four

An hour later, I sat on a fancy, white leather settee in the gallery, cradling a cup of Amy's bistro coffee. Red and blue lights from police cruisers outside cast a surreal, disco-like effect through the windows, making the remaining artwork on the walls look even weirder than usual.

"I can't believe you tackled a man with a gun," Liz said, perched next to me on the settee. She was still in her tie-dye dress, but had a silver emergency blanket wrapped around her shoulders. "That was brave."

"I can't believe your spell actually worked," I shot back. "Your powers are getting stronger by the day. It's been incredible to watch. A little scary, too, but mostly cool."

She grinned. "Turns out gallbladder surgery awakens all sorts of latent abilities. Did you know that in traditional Chinese medicine, the gallbladder represents anger? Maybe I was working out some of my perimenopausal rage. I have a lot of it, you know."

"Whatever it is, y'all are both pretty impressive," Amy drawled. She was holding a carafe of coffee and topped off our cups. She'd kept her shadow-melding hidden since the officials arrived. Still, the FDLE agents moving around the gallery kept giving us odd looks, but I couldn't bring myself to care. We'd just helped catch a pair of murderous art thieves. They could deal with some middle-aged witches.

"What's up with the tinfoil?" Amy said, gesturing to Liz's blanket.

"I'm cold with this air conditioning. Chris had this in the car. What? It's not used."

Amy shook her head and wandered off. Liz and I were left watching a CSI tech in a white jumpsuit dust for fingerprints on the doorframe.

"I'll bet that's an interesting job," she finally said, and I agreed.

Chief Chris Wolf approached, his usual stern expression a mix of relief and exasperation. Even though he wasn't officially on the case anymore, he'd shown up minutes after we'd called. He bent to kiss Liz's forehead, then gave me a look that clearly said, "this is all your fault."

As if I was the bad influence here. Sheesh.

"The FDLE are questioning Jack and Vanessa. Separately, of course." He pulled up a chair. "Want to hear what they're saying? I got some intel from a buddy of mine."

"I want to hear everything," I said, leaning forward.

He gave me a look that said, *of course you would.* "Dominic was getting sloppy with the forgery operation. Started sampling too much of his own recreational supplies. By that, I mean drugs, you copy? They were worried he'd expose everything."

"But why kill him at Pickled?" I asked. "Why not somewhere private?"

"Public place, lots of witnesses, easy to blame on natural causes." Chris shrugged. "Plus, they figured framing a local witch would throw suspicion off them completely. It's worked for them before."

"We know about the forged art," Liz said quietly. "Sophia told us about her grandmother's necklace."

Chris's head snapped up. "She what? When did you—" He stopped, pinching the bridge of his nose. "Never mind. I don't want to know. The less I know about whatever investigating you two did, the better." He shot me another accusatory look.

"Don't give Amelia that look," Liz said, reading his mind. "I'm perfectly capable of getting into trouble all by myself."

"That's what worries me," Chris muttered, but his stern expression couldn't quite hide his concern. He reached for Liz's hand. "You could have been hurt. Both of you."

"But we weren't," Liz said cheerfully. "And now the murder has been solved and Renee's name will be cleared, so everything worked out perfectly."

Chris sighed the deep sigh of a man who'd clearly given up trying to exert any control over his girlfriend. "The FDLE says Jack and Vanessa weren't small-time art thieves. They were working with an international ring specializing in stolen art and jewelry. Who in turn distributed forged and stolen art around the globe. Jack hasn't given up any names yet, though. We'll see when Interpol gets involved."

"What happens next?" Liz asked, squeezing Chris's hand.

"Now we've got two suspects in custody, evidence of multiple art crimes, and a very interested Interpol Art Crime Team headed our way." Chris shook his head, but I caught the hint of a proud smile. "Agent Martinez asked me to tell you she's officially cleared Renee of all suspicion. The FDLE's forensics team found traces of simple herbs outside the gallery. Some sage. Nothing sinister."

"Just Joey the ghost busboy moving on," Amy said smugly.

"Excuse me?" Chris said.

"Nothing," Liz and I answered in tandem.

I smiled, thinking of Renee, safe at Liz's house with the dogs. We'd have to fill her in on everything later, preferably over brunch and mimosas. For now, though, I was content to sit here with my friends, drinking surprisingly good coffee and basking in the satisfaction of a mystery solved.

Chris cleared his throat. "Promise me one thing? Next time you decide to investigate anyone, maybe give law enforcement a heads up first?"

Liz and I exchanged glances. "Define 'heads up,' " she said innocently.

Chris groaned and muttered something that sounded suspiciously like "I need a vacation."

The gallery doors opened, and Oliver appeared, looking rumpled and worried. His hair stuck up on one side, like he'd just woken up.

"Amelia!" He made his way over, past a crime scene tech. "I got your note. I'm so sorry. I sleep like the dead."

"I know you do," I said.

"Freddie had to knock a water glass off the coffee table to wake me up."

"It's okay." I said, rising to meet him. "Everything's fine."

He pulled me into a gentle hug. "I love you," he whispered against my hair.

"Love you too." I breathed in his familiar scent, feeling the last of the evening's tension melt away. "And don't worry about sleeping through the excitement. Between you and Freddie and Liz and the coven, I've got quite a protection squad."

I thought about everyone who'd helped us over the last week. Thompson with his security footage and bourbon-laced revelations. Amy and her shadow-melding. Donna sharing her mother's painful history. Even Jimbo, with his encyclopedic knowledge of deadly plants. Who would have thought that when I moved to Cypress Grove, I'd find not only a home, but a whole network of talented (yet extremely quirky) people looking out for each other?

Oliver chuckled and dropped a kiss on my forehead. "I have to admit, Freddie's turned out to be quite the alarm system."

"He's got his moments," I agreed, leaning into Oliver's embrace. "But I wouldn't trade either of you for anything."

Epilogue

About two weeks later...

The summer solstice festival transformed Bicentennial Park into a magical wonderland at dusk. Giant moonglobes — glass spheres filled with bioluminescent algae from the Gulf of Mexico — were scattered on tables around the lawn, their ethereal blue-green light pulsing in time with the ambient music. A few buds of night blooming jasmine had opened, and the fragrance mixed with sweet olive and magnolia to create an intoxicating perfume.

I smoothed my gauzy white dress and adjusted my flower crown. This one was much better than my previous attempt; the blooms were fresh and woven with actual skill by a local florist friend. Plus, no safety pins were involved in the construction of my outfit — and I hadn't gotten any of Amy's chili on my dress during our pre-event tailgate party in the parking lot. Progress.

The Wisconsin newlyweds from the inn walked past, hand in hand. The bride still had traces of blue glitter in her hair from her showgirl-themed bachelorette party. They'd extended their stay twice now, utterly enchanted by Cypress Grove. They waved as they found seats near the stage where the pardoning ceremony would take place.

Couldn't blame them for being enchanted. The town had

worked its magic on me too, in ways I never expected. A year ago, I was a divorced cookie company owner in California. Now? I was a legitimate witch who helped solve murders. Life was weird and wonderful.

Oliver appeared with two glasses of lavender lemonade, garnished with sprigs of mint. He looked particularly handsome in a linen shirt and his own laurel wreath. "They're about to start," he said, handing me a glass.

"Thanks." I took a sip, savoring the cool sweetness. We drank in silence for a few minutes, taking in the crowd.

"Hey," I said, spotting a familiar face in the crowd. "Is that Donna?"

Sure enough, Donna Anderson stood near the stage. She'd traded her usual cargo pants for a flowing black dress, but her steel-gray hair was still pulled back in that severe bun. For once, she wasn't radiating "don't talk to me" energy. Instead, she was deep in conversation with Marisol about medicinal plants.

"She's teaching a workshop next month," Oliver said. "Herbal medicine basics. It's already full, with a waiting list. Marisol told me when I ran into her at the lemonade stand."

I smiled, remembering her fierce protection of her plants. "No deadly species allowed, I assume?"

"Probably not. Her only stipulation is that she could bring her dog to the class."

"That's not a dog," I muttered. "That's a small horse who thinks he's a puppy."

Oliver laughed and pulled me closer. The gathering hummed with energy, both magical and mundane. We chatted for a few minutes about Sage, who had gotten the paralegal job.

"Jimbo's taking next week off so he can take her to some ranch in Montana to celebrate," I said, my voice fading as people began to take the stage. A hush spread through the crowd.

In the gazebo, Renee led a small choir in singing mystical solstice songs. The town's mayor and Donna stood to the side of the stage, listening with serious expressions.

I thought about everything that had happened: the visions, the confrontations, the triumph of women supporting women. We all did well. Renee, Liz, Amy, Donna. Though I could have done without almost dying in an art gallery.

In speaking of Amy, I spotted her in the crowd, talking to... Luca. I stifled a grin. Well. Perhaps a love match was underway. Good for them.

A few songs later, Liz joined us, her chunky crystal earrings catching the blue-green light from the moonglobes. She'd twisted her curly hair into an elaborate crown of braids interwoven with silver thread that sparkled when she moved.

"The energy here is incredible," she whispered. "I can practically taste it."

"Or your intuition is particularly strong tonight."

She grinned. "Chris says I glow in my sleep now. Actually glowing, not that pregnancy glow that everyone talks about. Can you imagine being our age and being pregnant?"

Oliver nearly choked on his lemonade and I snorted a laugh. I was about to ask where Chris was when he walked up and slid an arm around her waist.

"Sorry, babe. Had to take that call. It was Agent Martinez from the FDLE," he said quietly. "Jack and Vanessa have been moved to federal lockup. They're being charged Monday with forgery, conspiracy, murder. They're not getting out anytime soon."

"Good," Liz, Oliver, and I said in unison.

Mayor Samantha Chen stepped up to the microphone, and a hush fell over the crowd. Despite her youth, she commanded attention in her crisp linen suit and trademark red-framed glasses. At thirty-four, she was the youngest mayor in town history, and the first to openly practice witchcraft.

"My fellow citizens," Mayor Chen began, her voice carrying across the park. "We gather tonight not only to celebrate the solstice, but to acknowledge a dark chapter in our community's history. Sixty years ago, Constance Winters was wrongly accused of murder. She died in prison, away from her daughter, her craft, and her community."

A breeze stirred the jasmine, carrying its sweet scent across the crowd. The moonglobes pulsed slower now, their blue-green light dimming to match the solemnity of the moment. Even the ever-present Florida cicadas seemed to quiet.

"But Constance's spirit never died," the mayor continued. "Her legacy lived on in her daughter, Donna, who stands with us tonight."

Donna stepped forward, and for the first time since I'd met her, I saw her hands trembling. Rocky pressed against her leg, as if lending her his strength. The severe bun, the sharp angles of her face couldn't hide the tears in her eyes.

"In accordance with Florida state law, and with the full support of the governor's office, I hereby formally pardon Constance Winters of all charges." Mayor Chen's voice cracked slightly. "Let the record show that she was innocent. Let history remember her as she truly was: a healer, a mother, a protector of ancient knowledge."

Donna's shoulders shook as she accepted the formal document. When she spoke, her voice was barely above a whisper, but in the absolute silence, everyone heard her.

"My mother died alone because this town feared what it didn't understand." She took a deep breath. "But tonight, I see a different Cypress Grove. A place where magic is celebrated, not feared. Where justice, even delayed, still matters."

I felt tears rolling down my own cheeks. Oliver squeezed my hand. With my free hand, I reached for Liz.

"In her memory," Donna continued, stronger now, "I'm opening parts of the greenhouse for public classes. My mother believed in sharing knowledge, in teaching others about the healing power of plants. It's time I honored that belief."

Rocky let out a deep yet soft woof, and scattered laughter rippled through the crowd, breaking the tension.

"Though I'll keep the more interesting specimens under lock

and key," Donna added with a hint of her dry humor. "And Rocky will still be head of security."

More laughter, warmer this time. I saw Marisol dabbing at her eyes with a handkerchief, and even Chief Wolf looked suspiciously misty for someone who allegedly didn't believe in magic.

"Let this pardoning serve as a reminder," Mayor Chen said, "that our community is strongest when we embrace *all* of our citizens. Let it remind us that justice, while sometimes slow, is worth fighting for."

The moonglobes brightened suddenly, their light intense and pure. I wondered if Donna did that, or Liz. Really, it could have been any of the dozens of witches here in the park. In that moment, as the blue-green light washed over us all, it felt like Constance herself was present, finally at peace.

Since we were standing near the front, I caught Renee's eye. She beamed at me from her spot on the stage, looking radiant in a flowing purple dress. She and Bosco were heading to Vermont in a few days to see her family, something she said always made her feel whole.

"Life's too short to skip family rituals," she'd told me over coffee yesterday. "Even if my mother's idea of magic involves a lot more mushrooms and forest magic than I'm used to."

Her laughter had been genuine, free from the strain it had carried during the investigation. The whole ordeal changed her, but not in the way you might expect. Instead of making her bitter about dating and men, it had somehow freed her.

"The funny thing is," she'd said yesterday, "being targeted actually helped me get over my fear of being alone. Here I was, thinking I needed a man, any man, for companionship. Then this silver fox shows up, and he turns out to be a murdering art thief with a secret wife. No thanks. I'm better off alone."

When the ceremony concluded, I noticed Sophia standing at the edge of the crowd. She looked different. More natural somehow, without her usual perfect makeup and designer workout clothes. She was dressed plainly, in a jean skirt, a T-shirt, and sandals. When she spotted me, she gave a small wave and walked over.

"I wanted to thank you," she said quietly. "For everything."

"How are you holding up?" I asked. The local gossip mill had been churning about her divorce from Richard, though details were surprisingly scarce.

She sighed. "Better than I deserve, honestly. Richard is kinder than I expected. Got me a lawyer who helped make my legal worries go away. The real necklace is still missing, probably in some collector's vault somewhere." She shrugged. "Maybe that's karma."

"I'm curious," Liz said, her voice neutral, "have you talked with the feds about Dom?"

Sophia nodded. "Everything I know about his operation, his contacts, the whole international network. It wasn't much, but I did what I could. Agent Martinez says my cooperation will count for something." She glanced around the festival, at all the families and couples enjoying the magical evening. "I'm moving back to Miami next week. Fresh start."

"Good luck," I said, and meant it.

She gave us a wan smile. "I meant to tell you, about that replica necklace? It's actually quite beautiful on its own. I couldn't see it before because I was so focused on what was lost." With a final nod, she melted back into the crowd.

"Well, that was unexpectedly profound," Liz murmured.

"No kidding," I said.

"Ooh, I think you're needed," Oliver said to Liz and I, gesturing around us.

A hush fell over the crowd as women began moving toward the center of the park. The moonglobes dimmed to a soft, ethereal glow as witches of all ages formed a massive circle. I saw familiar faces from shops and restaurants around town, plus others I'd never met but somehow knew were part of our magical community.

"Time for the circle," Amy whispered, materializing beside

me. Her shadow-melding was subtle tonight, just a slight shimmer around her edges that could have been mistaken for moonlight. "You ready for your first solstice ceremony?"

I nodded, suddenly nervous. Liz took my right hand, Amy my left. Oliver melted into the background with the other men. Around us, hundreds of women joined hands until the circle was complete.

From the gazebo, Renee raised her arms. The choir behind her began a low, haunting chant that seemed to vibrate through the earth itself:

As summer peaks and daylight reigns,

Magic flows through mortal veins.

Circle bound and circle free,

As we will, so mote it be

The words weren't in any language I recognized, yet somehow I knew them, as if they'd been sleeping in my bones waiting for this moment. Goosebumps rippled across my skin as the entire circle joined in, our voices rising and falling like waves.

The moonglobes pulsed brighter with each verse, their blue-green light creating shimmering patterns across the grass. The night-blooming jasmine, which had been mostly buds when we arrived, burst into flower all around us, releasing waves of sweet perfume. Even the ever-present Florida humidity seemed to pause, replaced by a cool breeze that carried hints of sea salt and wild magic.

Amy's hand was cool in mine, Liz's warm, and I felt the power flowing between us like an electric current. For the first time, I truly understood what it meant to be part of this community of women. We weren't merely a coven or a town. We were something ancient and powerful, connected across time to every witch who'd ever raised her voice in ceremony.

We looked out for each other. We cared for each other. We had each other's backs.

As the chant reached its crescendo, sparks of light danced above our heads like earthbound stars. Later, the non-magical folks would claim it was fireflies or trick of light. But we knew better. In that moment, as hundreds of voices joined as one under the solstice sky, magic was real and tangible and absolutely undeniable.

And I was part of it all.

When it was over, I embraced Amy (which felt like hugging a cloud, weirdly), and then Liz. Then I went to Oliver. My face felt flushed, and an ecstatic joy flowed through me. "Wasn't that incredible? I've never done anything like that. Never felt anything like that."

"It was impressive. Y'all sounded like angels. Did you see that light show?" He leaned down and kissed me. Longer than a peck, but not a full French kiss. Now I was even more flushed.

"Want to get more lemonade? They have a version with vodka," he murmured into my ear, his sexy dark stubble tickling my face. Little sparks of awareness went through me, as they always did when he was near.

I was so smitten with this man.

"That sounds excellent." We were about to walk off when a young woman stepped in front of me. Her green eyes were wild and familiar, and I gasped.

It was my daughter. *Jenny.* I opened my arms to hug her, and my mouth to ask her why she was here. And how she got here. And how she managed to find me at this festival in the park in a town she'd never set foot in.

But she seized my upper arms and shook me ever so slightly, fear etched on her face.

"Mom, what are you doing? Why are you wearing a flower crown? What were you chanting? Who is this...this dude with the glasses? Are you in a cult? Are you okay?" Her tone rose an octave, and people around us stared.

"Mom, what's going on in this town?"

—THE END —

Thank you for reading my book! Your enthusiasm and love for this series makes me so happy. I appreciate all of you.

I know I've left you on a cliffhanger, but not to worry! TOTAL ECLIPSE OF THE HEX is book six, and is available!

Book six of the Crescent Moon Mysteries is available. One-click TOTAL ECLIPSE OF THE HEX now!

But that's not all...

If you'd like to read more about Renee Zinn and her adventures in the Green Mountain State, read MAPLE SUGAR AND MAGIC, which is available in Kindle Unlimited!

Baz Halloway's Spiced Banana-Prune Muffins

Long before health food stores dotted every corner and "superfood" entered our vocabulary, Basil "Baz" Halloway was brewing up magic in his humble kitchen in Cypress Grove. A World War II veteran turned baker, Baz discovered the healing properties of prunes during his travels through Eastern Europe in the 1950s. He returned home determined to create treats that were both nourishing and delightful.

These muffins were his masterpiece, lovingly developed during full moons when he claimed the prunes' properties were at their peak. Local mothers swore his muffins cured everything from children's tummy aches to senior citizens' various digestive complaints. Baz would only smile mysteriously when asked about his secret ingredient, though many suspected it was the precise timing of adding the spices while humming an old Celtic tune.

When he passed beyond the veil during the Harvest Moon of '99, his recipe box was found with this single recipe inside. The box itself was made of rowan wood — a tree known for its protective properties. Some say that on quiet mornings, you can still hear him humming in the kitchen of his former home, and the scent of his spiced prune muffins drifts through the air right before dawn.

INGREDIENTS

- 1 cup prunes, chopped
- 1 cup water
- 1 ripe banana, transformed to mush (about 1/2 cup)
- 1/4 cup unsweetened applesauce
- 1/4 cup vegetable oil (or melted coconut oil for tropical vibes)
- 3/4 to 1 cup sugar (brown or white, follow your heart)
- 2 large eggs, fresh from the coop
- 1 teaspoon vanilla extract
- 3/4 cup all-purpose flour
- 3/4 cup whole-wheat flour
- 2 tablespoons ground flaxseed (optional magic fiber boost)
- 1 teaspoon baking soda
- 1/2 teaspoon baking powder
- 1/2 teaspoon salt
- 1 teaspoon ground cinnamon
- 1/2 teaspoon ground nutmeg
- 1/4 teaspoon ground cloves (for the brave)
- 1/4 teaspoon ground ginger (for the adventurous)

INSTRUCTIONS

Prune Potion: Begin your culinary sorcery by preheating your kitchen to 350°F (175°C). In your smallest cauldron (a pot), bring prunes and water to a mystical boil. Reduce the flames and let them simmer until they surrender their firmness (about 5 minutes).

Muffin Chamber Preparation: Arrange your 12-cup muffin vessel. Line with paper shields or anoint with oil.

Wet Ingredient Alchemy: In your largest mixing bowl, orchestrate a dance between sugar, oil, and applesauce until they become one. Crack open your dragon eggs and add them along with the vanilla essence. Finally, introduce the mashed banana to this gathering of moisture.

Dry Ingredient Ceremony: In a separate realm (another

bowl), unite the flours, flaxseed powder, baking minerals (soda and powder), salt crystals, and your chosen spice brigade.

The Great Merger: Carefully unite the dry realm with the wet kingdom, stirring until peace is achieved. Fold in your prune potion with any remaining elixir.

Portioning Ritual: Distribute your magical mixture among the waiting muffin chambers, filling each to about 3/4 of its capacity.

Transformation Time: Let your creation evolve in the heated chamber for 18-22 minutes, or until a wooden wand comes out clean when inserted.

Cooling Enchantment: Grant your muffins 5 minutes of contemplation in their pan, then relocate them to a wire rack for their final cooling journey.

The Final Spell: Once cooled, these prune-powered delights are ready to cast their spell on any lucky taster!

About the Author

Tara Lush is a Florida-based author and journalist. She's an RWA Rita finalist, an Amtrak writing fellow and the winner of the George C. Polk award for environmental journalism.

Previously, she was a reporter with The Associated Press in Florida, covering crime, alligators, natural disasters and politics. She lives on the Gulf Coast with her husband and dog.

Sign up for her newsletter and stay up to date on all of Tara's book news. You can also find her here:

Website: taralush.com

Facebook: LushBooks

Instagram: The.Book.Lush

TikTok: CrescentMoonMysteries

Bookbub

Acknowledgments

I want to dedicate a special thank you to Lou Harper, whose incredible talent as the cover designer for this series has brought the world of *The Crescent Moon Mysteries* and its characters to life.

Lou's artistry and creative vision made every book in this series visually stunning, capturing the essence of the story in a way words alone could not. Her passion and dedication to her craft were truly remarkable, and I feel incredibly fortunate to have had the privilege of working with her. Her humor was infused in every cover she designed.

Lou passed away while I was working on this book.

Even though I had never met her in person, her presence will be deeply missed. Her work will live on in every cover she created. This book is as much a testament to her creativity and spirit as it is to the characters and stories we all love. Thank you, Lou.

Tara's Titles

Crescent Moon Mysteries

Eat, Pray, Hex

I Want Your Hex

Every Hex You Take

Cattitude and Charms

Serving Up Hex

Total Eclipse of the Hex

Raiders of the Lost Hex

The Critters and Criminals Series

Gator Queen

Swamp Princess

The Coffee Lover's Mystery Series

Grounds for Murder

Cold Brew Corpse

Live and Let Grind

A Bean to Die For

9 798989 326976